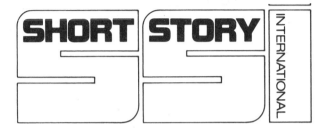

SHORT STORY SSI INTERNATIONAL

Tales by the World's
Great Contemporary Writers
Presented Unabridged

All selections in
Short Story International
are published full and
unabridged.

Editor
Sylvia Tankel

Associate Editor
Erik Sandberg-Diment

Contributing Editor
John Harr

Assistant Editors
Mildred Butterworth
Debbie Kaufman
Kirsten Hammerle

Art Director
Charles W. Walker

Circulation Director
Nat Raboy

Production Director
Michael Jeffries

Business Manager
John O'Connor

Publisher
Sam Tankel

Volume 14, Number 79, April 1990.
Short Story International (USPS 375-970)
Copyright © by International Cultural
Exchange 1990. Printed in U.S.A. All rights
reserved. Reproduction in whole or in part
prohibited. Second-class postage paid at
Great Neck, N.Y. 11022 and at additional
mailing offices. **Editorial offices: P.O. Box
405, Great Neck, N.Y. 11022.** Enclose
stamped, self-addressed envelope with
submission. One year (six issues) subscription
for U.S., U.S. possessions $22, Canada $24
(US), other countries $25 (US). Single copy
price $4.95 (US). **For subscriptions and
address changes write to *Short Story
International*, P.O. Box 405, Great
Neck, N.Y. 11022.** *Short Story
International* is published bimonthly by
International Cultural Exchange, 6 Sheffield
Road, Great Neck, N.Y. 11021. Postmaster
please send Form 3579 to P.O. Box 405,
Great Neck, N.Y. 11022.

Note from the Editor

This year, 1990, has been named The International Literacy Year by the United Nations, and efforts in many countries are focusing on alerting people to the importance of reading—the very core of education—in successfully surviving in our fast changing societies.

International Literacy Day, the United Nations' opening program for The International Literacy Year, was held on September 8, 1989, at the impressive UN headquarters in New York City. Among the participants were Barbara Bush, delegates from many countries, and 150 New York City school children under the age of twelve.

The program included three readings by authors. We are very proud that all three selections were from our *Seedling Series: Short Story International*, which is directed to 10-12 year old persons. Teruko Hyugo of Japan read her story "My Sister and My Headaches," Talat Abbasi of Pakistan read her story "Proper Shoes for Azam Khan" and Angela Marie Ferraiola of the USA (she is also a New York City public school teacher) read her story "The Best Kind of Eyes." As a measure of their quality, the stories charmed the adults equally with the children; a la Gertrude Stein: a good story is a good story, is a good story.

We believe a great number of people in the USA are still not aware that the USA literacy level among the nations of the world has dropped, and that literacy has a direct relationship to school success and the economic welfare of the individual...and the nation. After World War I a fourth grade reading level was adequate to earn a living in the USA, but today, as we continue growing more technologically complex, a high school reading level is required.

We believe that a lifelong habit of reading, with all its concomitant benefits, can be started by introducing engrossing contemporary short stories to people at any age and, therefore, we take this opportunity to suggest a look at pages 159 and 160 of this issue which carry our coupons for *Short Story International*, for *Student Series: Short Story International* and for *Seedling Series: Short Story International*.

Copyrights and acknowledgments

We wish to express deep thanks to the authors, publishers, translators and literary agents for their permission to publish the stories in this issue.

"Mountains Green and the Shining Stream" by Cheng Naishan from *Chinese Literature*, 1988. Translation by Lloyd Neighbors. By permission. "Garbage Girl" by Denys Johnson-Davies appeared in *London Magazine*. Copyright Denys Johnson-Davies. "Passing Glory" by T.G. Nestor, 1990. "The Ransom" from *The Wine-Dark Seas* by Leonardo Sciascia. Translation by Avril Bardoni. The story originally appeared in *Il Mare Colore del Vino*. Copyright © Giulio Einaudi editore. Torino 1973. Translation © Avril Bardoni 1985. By permission of Carcanet Press. "The Kingfisher: an Ecotheological Parable of Our Times" by Joseph John. Copyright 1990 Joesph John. "People of Consequence" by Ines Taccad-Cammayo originally appeared in *Solidarity*. Reprinted by permission. "The Dreams of God's Children" ("Marzenia dzieci bozych") by Julian Kawalec appeared in *Polish Perspectives* 1987. Translation by Edward Rothert. By permission. "El Circo" by Pedro Juan Soto, translated by Alfred J. MacAdam, appeared in *Review 33*. Copyright © 1984 The Center for Inter-American Relations, Inc. "The Tiger" by S. Rajaratnam from *Singapore Short Stories Vol. 1*, ed. Robert Yeo. Copyright © 1978 Heinemann Educational Books (Asia) Ltd. "Alien Corn" by Joseph Patron, 1990. "Big Dog" by Norman Lavers appeared in *The North American Review*. Copyright Norman Lavers. "Home" by Ales Rybak from *Soviet Literature*, 1986. Translation by Diana Turner. By permission.

Photo credit: Pedro Juan Soto by Ivonne Sanevitis.

Table of Contents

"I can say that we kids had no idea
the term 'half breed' was insulting."

Mountains Green and the Shining Stream

CHENG NAISHAN

THREE-seven-seven-four-zero-zero. I gently dial the number. At this time of day the sound of a phone being dialed is especially crisp and clear. I like to call you now, when the world's not yet awake. No, it wasn't my years working as a writer that made me an early riser. From the time I was born, I simply loved that intoxicating moment when the sun is about to rise. At that moment the very quietness of the world is bewitching. A milk cart chances by; the bottles clink together, and the sound wafts up like clear and melodious ice-crystal chimes; quivering, just at that moment when the first rays of the morning sun are about to appear, the lingering sound winds itself around just so, adorning the world that will soon wake from dreams to reality.

At that time of day no one notices me, no one cares about me, no one bothers me. At that time I'm completely alone, but this is just a fleeting impression, and precisely because it's fleeting, I value it even more—a special gift from the natural world.

377400. I twist the dial. It's certainly eye-catching, this attractive big red telephone with its white cord. Friends call it my "Fire Brigade Phone." I chose that color because I had a big red toy telephone when I was a child. Do you remember? It, too, had a dial that would turn, just like a real phone. Even though that toy phone had only a white string in place of a cord, I believed absolutely that I could use it to call anyone I wanted to. Later, after I grew up a little and studied something about electromagnetics, I still quietly dialed my toy phone and talked to you, earnestly hoping you could hear all I said.

37740. As I repeat this number over and over to myself, it gradually becomes "mountains green and the shining stream"—not a bad line for a poem, is it? (In the original Shanghainese the telephone number, read over and over again sounds like a line of poetry.) Feelings are remarkable things. They're like the magic wand in fairy tales. One wave of the fairy godmother's wand and a pumpkin becomes a glittering gilded carriage, the worn old shoes become dazzling little glass slippers. Just so, an insipid meaningless phone number takes on the beauty of a poem! 37740—"Mountains green and the shining stream." If you set it to music, like this: 3 - - | 7 - 7 | 4 - - | 0 - 0 |, and whistled the tune, it would have a certain allure. When I was a kid, I always whistled. Even now I secretly do it every once in a while. Naturally, I only whistle when it's quiet, when there's no one around to be bothered. Funny, isn't it, that someone my age should have such silly notions, should behave like a giddy young girl?

I open the curtains and look out through the misty windowpane over toward where you live. Your house is to the west from my window. At odd intervals lights flicker on in the little houses that stand out against the gray sky. There are other early risers. Are you awake now? Do you usually sleep on your left side or on your right?

Unconsciously I move my hand across the misty windowpane, and without realizing it, I've written your name—and mine. Long ago, when I was a skinny, little girl, my hair done up in funny pigtails, the popular "bean sprout style" of the 60's, I used to write your name on my window and in my copy book and in my diary, too.

I wasn't a diligent student. When I finished my homework, I loved to look out of the window. Almost anything would rouse my avid curiosity: the ceaseless movement of the clouds, lazy cats lying in the sun, leaves flashing in the sunlight. I liked to look out the window and absently whistle a tune. At that time I especially enjoyed whistling "Lovers' Melody," a song you always sang. As I whistled the melody, I'd think of the words I couldn't bring myself to sing: "...From this day on, we'll be together, I love you, my dear..." In those days I only needed to hear the roar of your Czech motorcycle in the alley and I'd race down the stairs to stand by the mailboxes in the stairwell, pretending I'd just come to fetch a letter, hoping you'd see me and exchange a few pleasantries. Usually you'd flash a quick smile and dash up the stairs, taking them two and three at a time. You couldn't possibly have taken notice of me, a sallow, skinny, little girl with her hair done up in laughable "bean sprouts," wearing a coat two sizes too large—to cover up her slowly ripening breasts. Why, you were stylish and free then, wearing your university student badge—admittedly the best-looking young man in the Lilac Villa Apartments.

Our names on the window gradually become blurred and disappear, turning to drops of water that slowly run down the pane. I blow on the glass and in the circles of frost draw a naughty little kitten.

I pucker my lips and softly begin to whistle "Farewell," a song that's flown across every street and alley of Shanghai, a song that's been whistled and strummed and hummed all over the city. It never occurred to me that the song was yours. I knew you were a singer but didn't know you were a composer as well.

"...Never knew parting would be so hard. Wish we'd never met..."

I whistle your "Farewell" and from time to time reach out my hand to the chilly wind, a wind that brushes so softly across my palm. I do this to prove my affection, to prove that all this really did happen.

This fall I came to your music troupe, full of curiosity, humming the song "Farewell." As a reporter from the arts section of

Newspaper X, I'd come to interview the composer of that song. I expected that she, "Mimi," would be delicate (since the melody of "Farewell" was soft and unbroken like the slender threads that silkworms spin), young (otherwise, how could she have described so accurately the joys and sorrows of young love?) and, of course, beautiful. (Mimi is, after all, a sensuous-sounding name. I remembered there was once a girl named Mimi who lived on our street. She was like a live doll, so pretty, but intuition told me she couldn't possibly write music.) The song was so full of sentiment, innocence and pain, it hooked onto my past and lifted it back before my eyes. My past has a lot of you in it...But you wouldn't know about that. On the way to your office, it was as though I were in a state of reverie, my mind somewhere else. On the tram I caught my stocking on the corner of a seat and got a runner. I'm often like that. I love to daydream, and when I do, I may trip over myself, even though the ground's perfectly level. At times like that, friends walk right by, and I don't even notice.

As I reached the gate of the Music Troupe offices, I saw you. Back toward me, you were squatting down, polishing a shiny black motorcycle. Being a reporter, I had learned something of the world and could guess that your big, eye-catching motorcycle was at least 350cc, not something you see often on the streets of Shanghai. It seems you'll never break your addiction to having a classy set of wheels. Yes, that was you all right. You were wearing a khaki shirt and faded blue corduroy jeans with a wide leather belt strapped around your waist. In the city this "Shanghai-style" dress is fairly common. But your physique immediately caught my attention. I hadn't realized just how deeply that form of yours branded itself into my mind. I have no doubt that out of a thousand, no ten thousand men, all dressed alike, I could pick you out in a glance. Is this, too, a kind of sorcery, like that of the fairy godmother and her magic wand?

We had been neighbors—upstairs/downstairs—at the Lilac Villa Apartments. Not till the "cultural revolution" drove us out of that beautiful lane did I realize the world was not what I thought it to be. Now, when I think back on those days in the Lilac Villa, it seems as though we were living in our own little Eden. That's where I drifted through the dreamy days of my teen-age years.

You were Eurasian, mixed-blood. I heard that your mother was a typist at the office of the Mobile Oil Corporation. Your father, or as you referred to him, "the man who conceived you," was an American employee at Mobile. Some of the old-timers around here said that after Pearl Harbor, when the Japanese marched into foreign concessions, your father was interned. At that time your mother was already pregnant, with you. It was then she moved into the Lilac Villa. Later, after the Japanese were defeated, the "man who conceived you" was released, unharmed, from the detention camp. But he didn't come to look for your mother; she and your father had never been officially married. My mother said that happened often in those days. Foreigners! He did give your mother a sizable sum of money, enough to support you in the Lilac Villa. He gave you this, in place of carrying out his duties as a husband and a father.

But we didn't concern ourselves with such complicated matters, for to children the world is simple. We saw that you looked like a foreigner, so we affectionately called you one. When we quarreled with you, though, we rudely called you "half-breed," a word we'd heard from some of those women who didn't have any feeling for your mother. In good conscience I can say that we kids had no idea the term "half-breed" was insulting. It's like when we yelled "I'm going to kill you" at someone. We weren't really planning to commit mayhem!

Though your blood was "half-imported," you weren't treated better than any of your little companions; maybe that's because our government's policy toward the outside world wasn't as finely drawn as it is now. You would get into fights just like other kids. And when your opponent got the best of you, he would sit on your chest and give you a few good licks. Even if you did have imported blood, it would never occur to a little boy that hitting you might have international consequences.

You were seven years older than I was. Ever since I can remember, I knew that you went by your mother's surname, you spoke Shanghainese at home, but with a Suzhou accent. You won second prize in the interscholastic Mandarin speaking contest, and around your neck fluttered the shiny red kerchief of the Young Pioneers.

We were neighbors. At one time you liked coming over to play. Do you remember that time you were so mean to me? On that day I had just gotten my big red beautiful toy telephone. I was excitedly playing with it in the flower garden on our lane. You came by.

That summer you were about to enter middle school. You were tall and skinny, like a matchstick with a gravelly voice. When you sang...no, even when you talked, your voice would squeak all over the place. At that age boys are like little banty roosters; it's an age when they arouse fear and disgust in the hearts of little girls and cats and dogs. Naturally, when you saw my toy telephone, you took it away from me. I was terrified you'd break it, what with your clumsy hands and feet. Standing on my tiptoes, I tried desperately to grab back the telephone, but then you spoke to me in serious tones, "Hey, I'll help you put through a call to Hades."

The hair on my neck stood on end. I stamped my feet in protest, but you paid me no heed, just pointed your finger at me and said mysteriously, "Quiet, or I won't be able to get through. Let me think. What is the Devil's telephone number? 131313. Just a minute. I'll dial it."

My skin crawled. I did, however, manage to calm down, overwhelmed both by fear and by your enigmatic manner. I watched you struggle to stick your fingers into the little holes on the dial. Boys your age always have dirty hands. Hangnails stuck up around the rims of your fingernails, nails that were all uneven, since you were in the habit of biting them. I was crushed that those hands would be touching my telephone!

You spoke with a ghastly voice into the receiver. "Hello, is this Mr. Ghoul?"

I was angry now. I didn't want to call the Devil on my telephone. That would be an insult to my lovable little toy. But you purposely dangled the phone just out of my reach and continued to wag your head back and forth, talking all sorts of nonsense. "...Afraid I can't come down there to play, Mr. Ghoul..." I ground my teeth in rage. I couldn't help it...I spat out a word I'd never used before, a word I'd heard other children use when quarreling with you: "Half-breed!" As soon as I'd said it, I was sorry. If you had lashed out at me like an angry young lion, if you had struck me a vicious blow, perhaps I wouldn't have realized so quickly how much I had hurt you.

But you just wagged your finger in my face and said softly, "Okay, so you're going to talk that way, too. Okay..." With that you gently placed that telephone on a rock in the garden and turned away.

Frightened, I looked at your face; it was black with anger. I pulled on your sleeve.

"Don't go. Play whatever you want. Tell me the Devil's phone number, and I'll dial it for you. Let's see, what was that number? It began with a one, didn't it?"

You didn't say a word. Just quietly lifted your arm, pulled out of my grasp, and walked away.

I was mortified. That night I lay in bed, still playing with my telephone, saying over and over into the receiver, "I won't ever call you 'half-breed' again." I really and truly hoped you'd forgive me. If you had just come to play with me again, you could've teased me all you wanted. I was convinced that telephone carried my words to you.

The next morning I woke to discover that my brand-new toy telephone had fallen on the floor; a piece of bakelite had broken off the receiver. Apparently I'd been making phone calls in my sleep.

You probably don't remember that incident as clearly as I do. It's been in my heart ever since. I hurt you, blamed myself for doing it, and suffered pangs of conscience. But, after that I never did get a chance to say I was sorry; you never came to play any more. This wasn't because you bore me a grudge. It's just that after summer vacation you suddenly became a man.

That summer, after I came back from my grandmother's, I discovered that you had changed, changed in ways that made you a stranger to me. Your voice was no longer gravelly, but rich and deep. That's right. From that time on the sound of a deep bass singing voice could be heard floating out over the sunporch. I remember it even now: the soft sounds of a guitar and a song from a Russian movie, *Lovers' Melody*. At first I thought it was someone playing a record, but then I discovered it was you. At that time I didn't quite understand what was happening...but I think I was precocious for a girl my age.

Your arms—no longer sticking out like skinny chicken legs—began to bulge and stretch the sleeves of your blue and white sweat shirt. The knuckles on your hands became prominent, revealing a masculine strength. From that time on I wouldn't have dared pull your sleeve again. I couldn't even look you in the eye. I somehow knew that you were moving toward the world of grownups, leaving behind the children, the children who shouted Mama this and Daddy that the whole day long.

Seeing you there once again, I instinctively went over to you, though I couldn't be sure you'd recognize me...For years I had been timid, lacking in self-confidence, beset by feelings of inferiority. But, after I'd gained a little experience of life, particularly after I had my reporter's ID in my pocket, after I'd published a few *stories,* even if these hadn't attracted much attention, I'd been able to gradually overcome my timidity and sense of inadequacy. Don't laugh at my childishness and self-satisfaction. I spent five years on a commune and three years welding coils in a community factory, had an abortion after four months of pregnancy, and then struggled through four years as an *overage* college student. When I think back on that, it wasn't easy!

Slowly you turned and squinted your eyes at me, a puzzled look on your face. You...you didn't remember me.

From that last time when we had bumped into each other on the street, ten years had flashed by. I had changed a lot. Thank God, those changes had been for the better.

The feeling of confidence and self-worth my reporter's ID gave me crumbled under your gaze. Lowering my head in embarrassment, I discovered a long runner shining prominently in the sun on my left stocking. I frantically tried to hide my leg behind the right one, but in doing so lost my balance and almost fell down...So, right in front of you, I made a fool of myself.

You recognized me, and not only called out my name but remembered the names of the stories I'd written.

"And now, you're working for..." he tried to guess.

"I'm a reporter for Newspaper X," I answered, rather proud of myself. I was delighted the day had finally come when I could show you I was no longer a timid, talentless little girl, that I had a profession and world of my own.

I didn't ask how you had come to work at the music troupe. I remembered that your major in school had nothing to do with music, but it didn't surprise me to find you working here. During the "cultural revolution," the ten years of chaos, people like us were arbitrarily swept up into the center of the storm. Then one day the winds stopped. It was like the little girl in *The Wizard of Oz*. The cyclone picked her up, along with her little frame house, and where she landed...well, that was where she landed. Fortunately you and I seem to have come out of it right.

"I like reading your stories," you said. "They tell all about the people and the happenings at the Lilac Villa. The old watchman, Mrs. Shen who lived at apartment number 8, even the curly-haired dog at number 3—why, they're all there. The only one missing is...me. It looks as though you've forgotten all about me."

I started to open my mouth to defend myself, but gave you instead a what-else-can-I-say smile.

"Wow! A little girl changes fast."

As you spoke, you never stopped sizing me up. It was clear from your expression that you were astonished. Of course some nice clothes and a little makeup, appropriately applied, are powerful aides, good news for a woman who's not really beautiful.

An indescribable happiness bubbled up inside me. I now had the courage to look you in the eye. You were standing with your back to the sun, so I had to squint my eyes, dazzled as they were by the light. Ah, the idol of my childhood. Neither the passage of time nor the changes of the world had tarnished you. It was comforting to know that my memory of something good and true had not been wrong.

"Did you come to see me?" you asked, tilting your head to the side, a slightly humorous tone in your voice. What? You think I made a special trip just to see you?

"Don't look so smug," I retorted bluntly. "I'm not just an empty-headed little girl with a pretty face." But you, well into your forties, still have a full head of black hair, curly and tinged with yellow. Your broad, unworried brow has two furrows running across it. There are crow's feet at the corners of your eyes—of course, wrinkles on a man's face, like dimples on a young woman's, only add to its charm. When you smile, the wrinkles at the corners of your mouth broaden; the dimples appear and then disappear...A casual open collar reveals your neck and shoulders, still firm and powerful. To tell the truth, even now you could be the object of any young girl's fantasies.

I haughtily straightened my shoulder-bag. "I'm here to interview the composer of 'Farewell.' She is now..." Though I was delighted by this chance encounter, I didn't want to make that too obvious. Just my woman's vanity acting up, I suppose.

"Well then, you really have come to see me!" You leaned against your motorcycle, arms folded, like a knight with his favorite horse, a look of satisfaction on your face.

I didn't understand.

"Mimi and me, you might say we're one and the same. She's me, and I'm her. Long ago she became a part of me, heart and soul, so to speak." I must've looked befuddled for you couldn't help but laugh. Tapping me on the shoulder as though I were your little brother, you said, "I'm Mimi. That song 'Farewell'—I wrote it."

"But, how?..." I couldn't believe it.

"Simple. I first wrote that song on music sheets mimeographed at the troupe. Then I lent it to a singer of our choral group; that's how it got sung the first time. Then during one performance one of our most popular singers got called back for eight encores. By the eighth encore he didn't have any other songs left, so he sang 'Farewell.' That's how it became popular."

This still seemed like an unlikely story to me. "But at the university you studied civil engineering, didn't you?"

"How'd you know that?" You stared at me in amazement. You never knew I paid so much attention to your comings and goings.

"I didn't really have the chance to learn much. My freshman year the Four Clean-ups Campaign was in full swing. The second year I did manage to get some studying in. Then, halfway through my third year, I bumped up against the 'cultural revolution'...I had a little trouble. Maybe you heard about that? I was arrested as a counter-revolutionary student—an active counter-revolutionary. So I was sent to prison for a number of years. Because of that I lost my status as a student and missed job assignment. I could try to get reinstated. But as far as my education is concerned, a diploma would be meaningless. I never learned anything at the university. It's better for me to be here with this music troupe. Music was my hobby, something I loved to do in my spare time, but that love has turned out to be the best teacher of all."

"I knew you were in trouble. That's over now, but I'm still curious about one thing: how did you get branded as an active counter-revolutionary?"

"Just for saying a few little sentences. I said, 'Lin Biao looks like a traitor. He's not a good man. If he rises to power, we'll all suffer.'"

"Did you really say that? Where did you say it?"

"In my dormitory room, talking to classmates..."

"You did that!"

"Stupid, wasn't it?"

We looked at one another and burst out laughing until sadness replaced our mirth. "In those days we weren't used to lying," you said, a bitter smile flashing across your face. You reached up your hand and pushed back a lock of hair, as though to wipe away the scars left by those unhappy times.

"Afterwards, how did you manage to get assigned to the music troupe?"

"Through my 'imported' blood," you said sarcastically. "I got special treatment for that. I'm responsible for taking care of the musical scores and other materials. At first I was disgusted with myself for being so low, for using 'the man who conceived me' as a way to get into the troupe. But then I thought: I was wronged and suffered greatly because of that blood he gave me. Now I'm getting some benefit from it, just to balance the scales. To tell you the truth, though, the way they're looking after me now...sometimes it's overdone. Makes me feel embarrassed. Of course, there are times when I have problems. For instance, taxi drivers, thinking I'm a foreigner, insist I pay them in foreign exchange certificates."

"Oh, you have a visitor!" A man greeted you as he passed by, at the same time sizing me up.

"Some people still think I'm like the guy who gave me half my blood, a born womanizer." You laughed and said, "It's as though I were making an advertisement for myself, standing in the doorway and talking. Let's go into my office and sit for a while."

As I walked along, I once again felt that runner down my ankle, but there was no way I could hop along to keep you from seeing it. You noticed I was walking a little strangely and asked considerately if my shoes were too tight. I could only pretend you were right. You gently took me by the arm.

"Don't..." I said. "You don't want to give people reason to say you're playing around with women again."

"Careful you don't twist your ankle," you answered, full of concern, carefully and stubbornly taking my arm again. I relented and leaned against your shoulder, my head just reaching up to that level. Just then it occurred to me that back when I was a pathetic little girl with my hair done up in "bean sprout" braids, I desperately wanted you just to look at me, would've given anything for such a look. But that never happened.

In the distance someone was out on the field doing his voice lessons, singing "Moscow Nights." Suddenly, I thought of something.

"Do you remember 'Lovers' Melody'?" I said, raising my head and looking at you.

"You know that song, too?"

You didn't expect that either, did you?

"Don't underestimate me," I said jokingly.

"It's not that. I was just thinking you were pretty young then."

It's true. I was young. But, when you stood on the terrace and sang that song, you were singing to me, a girl who was growing up, and early on you left me with a restless feeling of waiting for something, hoping...

"Those days I always heard you singing that song. Sing it for me again now." I even scared myself when this last sentence popped out. My heart was pounding.

"I haven't sung that song in a long time. Don't know if I still remember the words." Your deep-set eyes gazed into space for a minute, a sweet, innocent smile curling around the corners of your mouth. "Lovers' Melody" had some hidden significance for you—as it did for me. But in your case that significance had nothing, absolutely nothing, to do with me.

At that moment an inexplicable sadness came over me. Don't laugh.

"When I was young, I had a friend. Barefoot and pale of face, he followed me everywhere..."

Softly you began to sing. You turned to me with a delighted, childlike expression on your face, as if to say, "My memory's not bad, is it?" I couldn't help but hum along.

Your office was in the courtyard of the music troupe, in what had been the garage of a Western-style house. This tall, spacious building had been partitioned into two floors. On the ground floor were stacks of musical instruments waiting for repair and various music stands with broken arms and legs. Your office was on the second floor. As we walked together up that narrow staircase, your hand gently took hold of mine. Your idea was to keep me from falling, but our hands touched just as we were singing "Lovers' Melody," and so we walked on up the stairs holding hands and swinging them to the beat.

"...From this day on, we'll be together, I love you, my dear..."

I sang the words along with you. Nothing could have seemed more natural or full of feeling.

"Ah, good. There's no one here," you called out happily as you opened the door. "We can have a heart-to-heart talk."

Your tiny office was packed with bookcases. Near the window two desks had been placed facing each other. On one of these desks sat a dirty old artificial leather satchel. The other desk was spotless. and orderly. Underneath the glass which covered the top of the desk was a three-dimensional picture of Big Ben and a photo of Placido Domingo hitting a high note. Right in the center was a picture of a naughty little kitten, looking out with its head cocked to the side. Above the cat, looking as though they were written by a child, were printed the English words, "I miss you." My intuition told me this was your desk. I sat down alongside the desk.

Just right! With my finger I tapped on your glass tabletop.

Through the open window, as on a television screen, appeared a corner of the cloudless azure sky. The top of a magnolia tree reached up to the level of the window. Rays of the midday sun flashed and leaped through the gaps in the leaves. The sun was dazzling, the leaves a kingfisher green, and the sky a crystalline blue...a beautiful world.

And yet, the air was filled with a smell not quite so pleasant, the smell of fish. I quickly discovered the source, two scaled and gutted fish on the windowsill, in the sun. Seeing me glance that way, you leaped up, raced over to the window, and carefully took the fish off the windowsill. Giving them a little sniff, you mumbled, "I forgot about them. They almost got baked in the sun." You hung the fish in a shady place, explaining to me, "Behind our compound is a market. During the lunch hour it's convenient for me to slip over there, look around, and buy some food."

"Your...ah...your wife, what does she do?" I just had to ask.

"Accountant," you said simply, condensing your answer, as though you were drafting a telegram.

"How did you fall in love with her?" I asked, with a purposely mischievous tone to my voice.

"When I got out of prison, a good-hearted neighbor did her best to find someone for me. She's a fine woman..."

I wasn't sure whether "fine woman" meant your wife or your neighbor. I didn't ask.

"And you? How'd you meet your husband?"

"Oh, he's in the army, a cadre's son."

"And how did you fall in love with him?" You winked, showing that you were teasing me.

"Well, I'm not even sure..." I stammered, rambling on incoherently. "At first, I didn't believe it could be possible for me; our backgrounds were so different. I remember that there were some cadres living in the Lilac Villa. Even the slip covers for their sofas were People's Liberation Army green...At first I didn't think I could get used to such a life...We were together in the commune; spent four years there. Then one day he wrapped me up in his big green army overcoat. That's when I discovered I loved him...When

I was little, I saw a poster of 'Othello.' Do you remember that poster? This giant of a man, Othello, is wrapping his mantle around the delicate Desdemona. From that day on I was waiting for the day when a man would wrap me up like that, take me away from my loneliness and solitude, make me feel warm, give me someone to lean on..." I hesitated and looked at you uncertainly. Everything I had said was true, yet I was afraid you'd think I was making it up. At times my thoughts were so confused I didn't know whether to believe them myself. But I was speaking the truth.

You reached out gently and put your hand on mine. Your deep-set eyes slowly blinked, showing that you understood. That day your hand was immaculate, of course. The pores of your skin were large, and your hand was very white.

Someone came in the door. We hastily drew back our hands. The newcomer was a little old man in his fifties. Eyes ever vigilant, he studied me...and you.

"A reporter from Newspaper X," you said, introducing me.

The man gave a queer little snort, once again looked suspiciously around the room, picked up his satchel from the desk, and went out, purposely leaving the door open.

"Is anything wrong?" I asked, looking to you for help. That man's gaze gave me cold chills.

"What do you mean, 'Is anything wrong?' What's with you?" You answered bravely enough, but the tone of your voice revealed that the man had made you uncomfortable, too.

"Where were we?" you said, tapping on the desk top.

"We were just talking about each other, our experiences," I said blandly, cradling my chin in my hands. Though the old man was gone, something about him lingered on. It's like when a person is worried that polluted air will damage the young roses in his garden—I could no longer bring myself to talk about personal matters, about Othello's mantle.

I sat silent for a moment and then said, "I didn't expect you'd still be in Shanghai. I thought you left long ago."

In my circles the word "to leave" means "to leave China."

"Pick up and move my whole family to a strange country, start all over from scratch—that would be an enormous decision. I haven't made up my mind yet. You know, I just blinked my eyes and I'm middle-aged. The last ten years or so, with its terrible storms, I couldn't find shelter. Now, after a good deal of effort, I've got myself a place to live, been rehabilitated. I've established myself, settled down. I don't want to leave, not yet." Hearing these heartfelt words, I felt warm all over. Though we'd been out of touch for years, we hadn't grown apart.

"Oh, yes, do you still remember Mimi?" you asked. "Number 16. She did manage to 'leave.' She's a very determined woman."

Of course I remembered Mimi; she was known as the most beautiful girl in Lilac Villa.

"Yes," I said, "Mount Everest."

"Mount Everest?"

That's simple. You and Mimi were the same age. We little girls, our chests still flat as a boy's, were incredibly envious of Mimi, with her full, high breasts. So behind her back we gave her the nickname Mount Everest.

"Ah...Mount Everest!" You finally caught on and began to roar with laughter, tears coming to your eyes. I was actually a little embarrassed at this. I bent my head, cheeks flushed. The kitten on your tabletop stared out at me in warning, its little head tilted to the side.

"She's been gone three years already," you said, your words tinged with melancholy.

"Apparently even before the 'cultural revolution,' say 1964 or '65, her family had already moved out of Lilac Villa. Did you stay in touch with her?"

"I wish I had," you sighed. "In 1965 her father had some trouble and was arrested. Mimi's family couldn't afford the high rent at Lilac Villa, so they moved out. As they were leaving, Mimi came looking for me. She just wanted a few words of comfort from me. Or maybe she hoped I'd continue to see her afterwards...But at that time I was too young, too arrogant and vain. I'm not proud of the way I behaved when I was young."

As you spoke, you softly tapped your forehead with your fingers. "I was mad about another girl then; I didn't say a single comforting word to Mimi." You lowered your head. A shadow of pain flashed across your face.

Your words shocked me and made me understand something I hadn't realized before.

You continued. "Mimi left Lilac Villa in a state of despair, lonely and humiliated. Not till 1966, when I was driven out of our apartment, did I get a taste of what she had gone through. On that day my mother and I got up very early. It wasn't easy for us to hire a cart. We crept out of Lilac Villa, the place where I'd grown up. We were alone, not a soul to send us off..."

As you talked, you became more and more emotional. Your voice became husky, till finally you had to clear it with a cough.

You were wrong. That day you moved out, I was standing on the terrace, watching you and your mother...Your mother's hair, which had always been so black, seemed to have turned gray overnight. It had been chopped off, as though some old dog had chewed on it. You were straining to push that bicycle cart, piled high as it was with those household items you absolutely needed. Back hunched over with strain, you had lost that heroic air of the days when you sat astride your motorcycle. Your body looked exhausted, weighed down. You walked down the deserted alley and into the distance. You left early because you didn't want anyone to see you, isn't that right? Suddenly, it occurred to me that you shouldn't have to leave alone like that, with no one to send you off. I tore open the front door and raced down the stairs. But by the time I got out the front gate, your cart had long since vanished. Two months later my family was driven out of Lilac Villa. I don't know whether anyone saw us off in silence, saddened by our departure. I suspect not.

My eyes brimmed with tears.

"Let's not talk about the unhappy past," you said apologetically. You misunderstood why I was crying, but I didn't try to set you straight.

"Time does pass quickly. Just look. Since we left the Lilac Villa, twenty years have gone by in a flash, twenty years since we last saw each other..."

"No," I said. "During that time we did meet once."

"Really?" You had completely forgotten.

It was not long after Lin Biao had been killed. Probably you'd just gotten out of prison. We were on Nanjing Road. You called out to me.

"I'm okay now." Those were the first words you spoke to me. Why did you say them? I guess you hoped that through me your words would get passed on to all your acquaintances, and to those close friends who knew you had gotten into trouble. Now you were "okay." My, what a strange time that was!

"Ah...That's good," I stammered. By that time I had changed my hair from "bean sprout" braids to the Jiang Shuiying style. I was wearing an enormous blue unisex overcoat; it looked like a flour sack, covering up all the curves of my body. I'd lost my status as a student, lost my job, and lost my love. (If never having been loved is the same as losing one's love.) I was ashamed of myself for looking like such a fool. But, you...wearing your student garb of faded blue cotton, with your tiny gold insignia, your hair cut in a flat-top, like Japan's Admiral Yamamoto—even if your face was a little gaunt—you still looked stylish and handsome!

"Does your family still live at Lilac Villa?" You were holding a small bag of apples.

"No, we got chased out a long time ago."

I wanted to give you my address, but you didn't ask. I didn't dare bring it up myself. I figured you couldn't possibly have any interest in knowing where I lived.

"Are your father and mother all right?" you asked, shifting your weight to the other foot.

I nodded my head. I was too nervous, afraid you'd find me repulsive, afraid I'd do something to make you reject me. I acted as though I wanted to go.

You appeared to lose interest in talking to me, or maybe you misunderstood. Maybe you thought I was afraid to be in contact with you, for fear of getting in trouble myself. At any rate, you quickly brought our meeting to an end, but just as you were about to go, you picked an apple out of your bag and gave it to me.

That apple was ripe to perfection, so red it looked fake. First I rubbed it with my hands, then smelled it. Delicious fragrance! I put it up to my mouth and took a bite. The juice, sweet and tart, ran into my mouth. For the first time I thought: a lover's kiss must taste like this.

Naturally, as I told you about this earlier meeting of ours, I left out the part about the apple.

When I described how you were dressed, how you behaved, you were shocked.

"Your memory's incredible. But, why is it that whenever you saw me, you acted so ill at ease? We were neighbors, weren't we?"

"Because..." With my hand I traced the naughty face of that kitten under the glass. "Because I always felt you were so handsome, and I...so ugly!"

Ah-ha! You were embarrassed by what I said.

You laughed. Like a big brother you reached out and patted my hand, the hand that was tracing the kitten. "Are you afraid to sit here with me now?" Using the power of your seven-year age advantage, you thought to rescue yourself from embarrassment, but it didn't work. Between a man and a woman, seven years doesn't mean much.

I shook my head back and forth, smiling with delight. I was happy. Through my own effort I'd thrown off, forever, the problems that had plagued me since I was a girl!

"Have you been to Lilac Villa again?" you asked.

I shook my head no.

"I went back once, with Mimi," you said. "Just before she 'left' I went with her to see the old place."

Back to Mimi. "How did you run into her again?" I asked. I could feel that my question was charged with emotion.

"I met her on the street, just like I did you."

No, it wasn't like meeting me at all.

"At that time her daughter was already three years old," you added.

"So, do you write her often?"

"Rarely. At Chinese New Year's and other holidays we send cards. That's all."

"She sent that one," I said unhesitatingly, pointing at the kitten under the glass. It was an adorable cat, pure white, innocent eyes staring out...

"Last year at Christmas I got a fee for the song 'Farewell.' Add that to my bonus, and I had enough to call Mimi long distance."

"Wow! That's expensive!" I said, though it wasn't an appropriate comment.

You went on. "When she whispered hello, I didn't know what to say. So, I just sang to her over the phone, 'Farewell.'"

Beautiful. I closed my eyes and imagined what Mimi looked like, standing there listening to the telephone, beautiful in her American clothes. I envied her, was even a little jealous.

"What did she say?"

"She just cried."

I sighed and felt sorry for Mimi. Envied her as well.

"You like her." I paused and then corrected myself. "You love her."

You hesitated, denying none too firmly what I'd just said. "It's not THAT WAY at all. You see, I suffered so much myself, suffered because my father left me." Of course, how could it be THAT WAY between you two? I absolutely believed the last part of what you said. You were speaking from the heart. That's how "Farewell" came to be floating through every boulevard and alley of Shanghai. That's why you took the pen name Mimi.

"After we part, we still must laugh with the world.
Are you like me,
Laughing on the outside, crying on the inside?"

That's the refrain of "Farewell," with its solemn, sorrowful melody, the end of each phrase returning to an inevitable harmony. Right then and there, as I recalled the words of that song, a wave of bitterness rose up, filling my heart.

We sat there in silence, and in that lonely moment I felt a warm flow of tenderness in my veins. Dear friend, have you always faced the tests of fate alone and in silence? For an instant I wanted to cradle your head in my arms and press it softly to my breast. You were so close to me. I just had to reach out my hand and touch you!

"Hey, it's so dark in here. Why don't you turn on the light?" A sharp, woman's voice ruined everything. Her curious gaze fairly flashed around the room, taking in both you and me. Finally, she added in a loud voice, "Oh, excuse me...Don't mind me. I just came in to get some music scores. Actually, I don't need them right away..."

The overly-polite tone of her voice, the cunning expression on her face was hard to bear. Without waiting for us to speak, she left, tiptoeing out the door, acting as though some filthy secret, tormenting her conscience, had just been revealed. Unlike the old man who sits at the desk across from you, this woman pulled the door too gently, leaving it ajar. Immediately the sound of whispering came from the head of the stairs. Apparently more than one person was outside. Most likely, they'd been listening for some time and had sent her in to scout.

Only then did we realize that the sky was turning dark. The light from the setting sun could no longer illuminate our tiny room. Your body was just a blurry form in the twilight. I wanted to look at you again, but a cold wind blew in from through the unclosed door. Outside that open door, something was brewing, something dangerous, disastrous...I couldn't sit there any longer.

"Let's go," I said.

"Let's go," you said.

"Just a minute." I had just thought of something. I stepped behind the bookcase and quietly took off my nylon stockings. Then I looked into the glass door and straightened my hair. I had a premonition that when we said good-bye, it would be quite a while before we saw each other again—though it wouldn't be decades this time. I wanted to leave you with a good impression.

"This afternoon has been fun," you said, carefully wrapping up the fish in a music sheet. "It would've been good if we could've had this kind of open conversation earlier. I've been lonely."

"If we'd met earlier, we couldn't have been the same people we are today. Even if we were still neighbors, one upstairs, one downstairs, we couldn't have talked as we've done today."

"What you're saying is, life has changed us."

"Better say, we've grown up."

As we walked through the courtyard, I couldn't help but glance up and look longingly at that little window right on top of the garage. That was your office window. The rays of the setting sun swept a layer of rose-colored light across the window. That ordinary twilight seemed to me incredibly beautiful. Perhaps it would never be that beautiful again.

You pushed out your huge, shiny black motorcycle; it looked like a black stallion.

"A beautiful bike. You're never going to get over your addiction to those machines," I said, thinking of your old Czech motorcycle.

You stroked the handlebars. "If they let people ride horses in Shanghai, I'd definitely have one of my own."

I believe you. You would do that.

You put on your light-gray goggles. Suddenly you thought of something. "I'll give you my phone number: 377400. You want to write it down?"

"No need. I won't forget it."

"This afternoon was perfect. We had the chance to get to know each other again. But what about your interview? You can't make a report on what we've said."

I smiled and ran my hand lightly over the seat of your motorcycle. It was big enough to hold three riders.

You fished out your keys and got ready to leave.

"Wait a minute!" I suddenly reached out and grabbed hold of the handlebars. "Back then, when you lived downstairs, I longed for the day you'd drive me down the lane on your motorcycle...Why, whenever I heard the sound of your motorcycle, I'd race down the stairs and stand at the mailbox, pretending I just happened to be there...But you never even gave me a glance!" I forced myself to smile as I said this, but I could feel a lump rising in my throat. I could no longer control myself; I stopped, standing there in hopeless silence.

You got off the motorcycle, pulled off your goggles. We looked at each other for a moment, not saying a word.

"Get on. We'll drive by the Lilac Villa and take a look." You took me by the arm and helped me onto the seat, as though I were a helpless little girl. Flustered, I sat there, holding tightly to the edge of the seat. But you took my hands and put them around your waist. Your hands were warm and soft and moist. "Hold on to me," you said softly, firmly grasping my hands. I felt a warm breath of air brush across my cheeks. That was the fourth time our hands had touched that day, but this time was better than the others. That tender touch terrified me...and made me happy.

The cycle fairly flew, like a galloping stallion. The streets, the buildings, others cars swept past. This was the first time for me. I was frightened to ride like this, behind a man, on a motorcycle. I couldn't even ride a bicycle. I clung to you. The rearview mirror reflected my none-too-pretty, but contented face. It reflected, too, your face, serious, full of contemplation. I could see that behind those light-gray goggles your eyes were thoughtful. Marvelous! In the past I'd dreamed of this, but that dream could never come true. It was too far away, an extravagant, impossible yearning. But now...here it was. I felt the warmth of your body, heard two hearts beating, yours and mine. I couldn't hold back a little sob. With one hand on the handlebar, your other hand clasped mine that was clinging to your waist.

"Shall we hum a song?" you asked. "'Lovers' Melody.'"

We turned into Lilac Villa. The lane was covered with verdant bushes, a shallot green strip. Nineteen years ago I left this place. The Eden where I spent my childhood was still tranquil and beautiful. Soft yellow lights flashed out of the stylish, arched windows, casting slanted shadows on the verdant lane. The sudden sound of laughter floated out from one of the windows and twisted through the night. It was hard to believe a holocaust, a cataclysmic change had taken place here.

You braked to a stop at the entrance to number 10, our old building.

What if...what if...what if we were still neighbors, how would things have turned out?

From time to time people walked by, all strange faces. Few of our old neighbors, the ones we knew so well, still lived in Lilac Villa; that was for sure. That knowledge made us feel closer, for it seemed that we practically knew each other from the cradle.

"Let's go over to Mount Everest's window and take a look," I said.

Her window faced your terrace. No wonder you were always singing "Lovers' Melody."

The sound of a radio came from a window: "At the last stroke the time was exactly 7:00 p.m., Beijing Standard Time." That simple announcement brought a feeling of desolation into the quiet night. Time was flowing away, and all our nows would soon be a part of the past; but everything past, no matter how we change, will always remain a part of us.

It was late.

"I'll drive you home. It's no trouble."

"No, don't."

You didn't insist.

When I got down from that elegant 350cc cycle, I was like a child climbing off a carousel. I knew I had come back to the real world. Though I didn't want to get off, I knew there was nothing else to be done. A person can't stay on the carousel forever; the time comes when he has to get down.

You said good-bye.

Though we were standing in darkness, it suddenly seemed as though a great crowd of people was watching us. We donned our masks, became formal.

I walked away. I could feel that you were following me with your eyes, your mask pulled off. I turned the corner and then heard the sound of your motorcycle.

377400. I recited your telephone number to myself.

377400. I never did give you a call. Strictly speaking, I did call once, the very next day. I dialed the number, but as soon as the call went through and I heard your telephone ring, I...panicked. What if you weren't the one who answered?...Of course, that wouldn't really make any difference, would it? Whatever, I did lose my nerve. I hung up. Do you remember that? The phone only rang once, and then was silent. That was me! From that time on I haven't tried to call you again.

"Mountains green and the shining stream." That's when I began to have this powerful memory of my toy telephone, the one I played with as a child. I believed that only this little telephone had the magic power to keep secrets and to share messages from the heart!

377400. I twist the dial. After a second or two the crisp sound of a bell would begin to ring in your apartment. This early in the morning, the sound of a telephone would be sharp, even piercing. You'd be angry as you leapt out of bed, cursing, still in a sleepy stupor. Yet, you'd hurry, afraid of not getting to the phone on time, afraid you might miss...miss what?... At times there's no way to explain why we act the way we do. When we're at home and hear the doorbell ring, we would never let a stranger in and talk to him without knowing who he was. We wouldn't talk to him even if he were standing outside the door, presenting no threat to our home. But people who call on the telephone get special treatment. Even if we don't know who's calling, no matter how awkward the circumstances, we rush to answer, afraid the caller will get impatient and hang up. Who knows why this is true? Could it be we're half-consciously waiting for something, hoping for a change, waiting for the moment that will satisfy our yearning hearts, the moment that will make up for past disappointment?

However that may be, I won't bother you.

"Mountains green and the shining stream"—The world wakes and comes alive. When the curtain of a new day is drawn back again, we embrace that day, filled with hope. At dawn the land is full of hope and life, like an infant waking from sweet sleep.

I open the window and take a breath of sweet morning air. Then, looking west from my window—in your direction—say quietly, "Good morning, dear friend."

 *Born in 1946, Cheng Naishan graduated from Shanghai Educational College in 1965 and then taught at a middle school before becoming a professional writer. She has been greatly influenced by her parents who were university graduates trained in literature and music. Her writings are mostly based on Shanghai life, work and young love, and give insight into the Shanghai spirit and customs. Her story was translated by Lloyd Neighbors.*

"She was twelve maybe, maybe even less,
but in Western terms no longer a child."

Garbage Girl

DENYS JOHNSON-DAVIES

FROM time to time I lifted my eyes from the typewriter and looked down through the bare network of branches that later in the summer would be carrying a scarlet carpet of flame-of-the-forest. A few feet above the towering blocks of flats that stood along the banks of the Nile hung a biscuit-colored layer of pollution: a huge dome that acted like a mute to the sun's rays. Each time, when there was no sign of her, I returned to my work, but my mind was only half on it. It was the time of day, midmorning, when she and her young brother and the donkey cart would appear, though sometimes they would miss a day, not necessarily a Muslim Friday or a Christian Sunday. Then, suddenly, there was the sound of the bell. I jumped to my feet and there, four floors below, stood the rickety cart with its two sore-ridden donkeys. They were near the end of their round and the cart was almost filled with garbage. It was ringed with balancing cats who fought among themselves as they gingerly dipped their paws into the muck and sometimes succeeded in clawing up something to eat. I could see her young brother, his basket slung over his shoulder and almost scraping the ground, making his way from the large villa opposite and leaving behind him a trail of lettuce leaves and balls of soiled cotton wool.

She stood at the door, her half-filled basket at her feet. The dirty kerchief round her head I recognized as the piece of batik I'd once bought in Bangkok and passed on to her. With her pouty mouth she smiled at me. She was twelve maybe, maybe even less, but in Western terms no longer a child. Her large, beautifully shaped eyes demanded that she be thought of as a woman, a woman who was somehow able to appear detached from the reeking filth with which she worked. She was tall and thin and had a way of carrying herself that emphasized the nipples of two recently sprouted breasts straining against the stained *galabia*. Underneath it she was as naked as when her mother had brought her into the light, for once she had bent down and collected a couple of eggshells that had bounced off the edge of her basket, and the image of her light brown thighs and buttocks had stayed in my mind.

"*Shouf rigli,*" I heard her say and I brought my eyes down from her breasts to her feet. She lifted one foot and I saw that it had a piece of dirty rag round it.

"A bit of glass wounded me," she explained, dragging the rag aside so that I could see the deep gash in her instep. I told her to be careful about it, that I didn't have anything for it but that she should get some antiseptic. I turned away from her and searched in my pocket for a pound.

"Go to the chemist's after the *maidan,*" I told her, "and he'll give you something for it."

"It was a bit of glass," she said to me again, taking the note from me. I then remembered that I'd saved some sweets for her, so I went back into the living room and brought them to her. She pocketed them without enthusiasm; she knew them for what they were: the sweets that Cairo's groceries gave instead of small change now that piastre pieces had, with inflation, become worth more in pure metal than their face value. Some of Cairo's recent hard-faced millionaires who drove around in white Mercedes were making the money for their silk shirts and pointed Italian shoes from melting down these old coins. The grocers gave you small change in book matches or sweets, and since knowing Suha I'd been taking my change in sweets.

"Be careful about your foot," I told her again. "You should wear shoes," I added.

She gave me a look which said: I'll wear shoes when someone like you cares to give me a pair.

"One day, God willing, I'll give you some money for a pair of shoes."

"Don't you have an old pair?" she asked. "A pair you don't want?"

"They'd be too big for you," I said.

"Better than too small," she said with a laugh.

I remembered the pair of canvas shoes that were giving at the toes. They'd be double her size but she could slop around in them and they'd be some protection. I took them out from the bottom of the cupboard in the bedroom and handed them to her.

She examined them and put a finger through the hole in one of the toes as though to point out that in no way did they let me out of my promise to give her money for a new pair.

"Thanks," she said and put them on top of my garbage.

"You're passing by tomorrow?"

"God willing," she said. The smile she gave me seemed to suck me deep into her eye-sockets.

"God willing," I said and shut the door on her.

I stood on the balcony and watched her empty my garbage and that of my neighbors into the cart. As it moved down the street and turned into the *maidan*, the cats, finding themselves in foreign territory, jumped down. I returned to the typewriter and tried to continue with the piece I had a deadline on. Instead, I read through the last sentence, then sat back and lit a cigarette and thought that some day I should do a feature about Cairo's garbage people and the hundreds of donkey-drawn carts that collected it up and dumped it alongside the shanty town on the outskirts of the city. For years the government had been thinking of introducing modern refuse lorries and getting the garbage recycled as happened in every other self-respecting capital, but the figures never worked out right. How could you ever compete with the tribe of men and children who collected the city's waste in return for a minimal tip from the house-holder? They drove their carts in from the Mokattam Hills and their squalid shacks built around the heaps of rubbish. If, going out to the airport, you asked the taxi to take you by the Salah Salem route, past the Citadel and the Mohammed Ali Mosque, you could see the diminutive, overworked donkeys toiling up the steep slope before turning off to the Mokattam Hills. There the garbage people sorted through Cairo's refuse and fed part of it to the pigs they bred; it was said they were all Christians, Copts, for no Muslim would go anywhere near a pig, dead or alive. It was also said that only some-one who didn't know the conditions in which the pigs were kept and what they were fed would ever think of eating pork in Cairo. They excited sympathy from the foreign community, and the other day there was an item in the English paper about the ambassador's wife paying them a visit and that there was a sort of Sister Teresa who was devoting her life to them. All my Muslim friends said they didn't deserve any help and that they did very well from the strange monopoly they exercised. Perhaps there was a story there, per-haps one day I'd drive out to the Mokattam Hills and see for my-self. Perhaps I could arrange to visit Suha and her family there.

Can a man, a hard-bitten journalist, in what is euphemistically called middle-age, be in love with a refuse-collector of twelve? Can you really call it love? Many would call the emotion unnatural, a perversion, but they would be wrong. Maybe, though, it shouldn't be called love, for it's a sentiment more disturbing than that, a sentiment that hasn't as yet been given a name. Perhaps only certain people are prone to this special love/lust feeling. A man may live with a woman all the years of his life, he may have affair after affair, and yet never know this desperate pain that joins the heart to the crotch. To those who *are* prone to this bane, how often can it occur in a lifetime? To me it had happened three times before: once with the wife of my father's boss when I was fourteen and she getting on to her menopause; then, more recently with a Turkish Cypriot peasant woman who used to make *halloumi* cheese and had a shepherd husband who had done time in prison for knifing someone who'd made a pass at her. Then there was that woman who, sitting opposite with a teen-age boy, had shared a carriage on the underground with me between Russell Square and Green Park and had then stood on the platform and had held my eyes without risk till the train had disappeared on its way to Hyde Park Corner. And now there was Suha, the child with budding breasts and unfledged thighs, and a basketful of filth hung round her neck who daily rang the bell.

This unnamed emotion feeds and waxes fat on an exclusive diet of daydreams. As there is an unadmitted acceptance deep, deep down that where this emotion is at play fulfillment cannot be achieved, these daydreams are taken up to and beyond the borders of incredulity. Thus, ever since first setting eyes on Suha, I had rehearsed in my mind any number of possible and impossible situations between us: her taking a quick shower before joining me in bed, while her brother waited downstairs and wondered which flat she'd disappeared into; of her somehow escaping from her rounds and making her way secretly back to my flat for an hour, a night, a week. I even saw myself taking her in a taxi to the airport and catching the once-a-week Air France flight to Nice, having her dressed by the boutiques of the Riviera and walking with her along the Promenade des Anglais. The daydreams of self-fulfillment were neverending but so, too, were the *daymares* (have I coined a word?) of jealousy. Were there not others in whose hearts, as she made her rounds, she had awakened the same feelings, and had not some of them, bolder than me, won from her unthinkable favors?

I abruptly cut off the image of Suha standing naked under the needlepoints of water and forced myself back into the piece my paper had asked for about why Egypt's agriculture was all to hell since Nasser chased out the big landowners and built the Aswan Dam.

Two days passed without anyone turning up for the garbage. It had suddenly become warmer and the pong in the kitchen had begun to build up. Then, on the third day, there was a ring at the door and when I looked down into the street, the cart and the two donkeys were there, also her brother throwing stones at the scavenging cats. But at the door I was faced with someone I'd never seen before: a small man with a wall-eye. Though he looked too young, he told me he was Suha's father, that she was ill at home and that she'd been to the doctor who had said she needed her foot lanced but that he wanted five pounds for doing it. He said all this as though he'd learnt it by heart.

"I'm sorry to hear about your daughter," I told him and fished in my pocket and gave him a pound note.

"And the rest?" he said, cocking his good eye at the note. "Where will I get the rest from?"

I thought quickly, then took the pound from his hand and went to the bedroom and searched in my coat pocket. I returned with a five pound note and handed it to him. He looked surprised rather than grateful.

"May God grant you a long life," he said.

"May God cure your daughter," I said and brought him my garbage from the kitchen, then went back to my typewriter. I had sent off my piece on Egypt's agriculture and was now trying to write a final paragraph to my latest story, already overdue, about the political clout of the Muslim fundamentalists.

A week went by and the cart looked after by Suha and her brother was replaced by another one in the charge of two rough-looking, rough-speaking boys who looked like twins. I asked them about Suha but they said they'd never heard of her; I mentioned a young girl who'd cut her foot and they didn't know anything about her either. One of them took fifty piastres from me and came regular as clockwork daily at eleven; their donkeys were larger and better fed and had leather traces instead of the wire ones that bit into the flesh of Suha's skinny couple.

Then the man who said he was Suha's father called round again. He didn't try to deaden the blow but said straight out that Suha had died, that her foot had swollen more and more and that it had got gangrene, and she'd died. Now he wanted money for her burial. I gave him two pounds and shut the door on him. The rest of the morning I spent staring ahead of me into the branches of the flame-of-the-forest tree and wondering whether the garbage people used coffins.

It must have been two months later, it was high summer and the price of Teymour mangoes had come down to as low as they'd be.

I was walking through Maidan al-Misaha weighed down with two string bags of groceries. Shouts and a cloud of dust ahead indicated that a game of football was going on in the road that separated the two plots of coarse grass and sparse flowerbeds. As I jumped ungainly to one side to escape the ball I was sure had been aimed at me, I saw her sitting beyond one of the heaps of clothes that indicated a goal post. Stately as Cleopatra in her barge, Suha was sitting on the cart with her feet resting on the front nearside wheel. She was puffing at a cigarette and the smoke curled up in the still air forming a bluish-gray plume to the red kerchief round her head. Though her gaze was directed towards me she made no sign of having seen me. My heart began to beat heavily and I became conscious of the strings of the bags cutting into my palms. I braced my shoulders and tried to stride on as though oblivious of her presence, but as I reached the turning to my street I felt the strength go out of my legs. As though a great lump of cat's fur had lodged itself in my chest, I suddenly found difficulty in breathing. I had a moment's fear that this was how one felt when about to have a heart attack. I came to a stop and rested the carrier-bags on the ground. I glanced back at her and saw that she was looking in my direction. Her tall, upright figure was posed against the darkening sky; her hand with the cigarette was resting against her cheek. I took up the bags and walked forward several steps. When I looked round again she was blocked out by the new building of flats that was going up on the corner of the *maidan*. With a deep sadness, a nostalgia that was well familiar to me, I knew I'd never see her again.

Denys Johnson-Davies travels frequently from England to Egypt. He was born in Canada, spent his childhood in Egypt, the Sudan and Uganda and then studied Arabic at London and Cambridge Universities. Volumes of his stories and translations have been published. He has been a barrister in London, a lecturer at Cairo University and a director of an Arabic broadcasting station in the United Arab Emirates.

"Whatever it was before the corncrake shrilled,
whatever the mood held or was leading to,
was now all shattered and gone."

Passing Glory

BY T.G. NESTOR

IT had etched itself permanently in his mind. One main picture and
two lesser ones, like a triptych. It had seared and burned into his
brain, into a permanent archive in that part that held those things
that created deep, lasting impressions. He never knew for sure why
Rockbarton had qualified for such stark prominence in his mind. It
was seven years since he first saw it. He was twelve then, going on
thirteen. A gangling youth, carrying a homemade fishing pole,
rounding a bend of the River Deel. Of course he had heard of the
place. Rockbarton was deep in the folklore and in the reality of his
environment. It stretched back three hundred years or more, to
when Elizabeth I had granted a tract of remote Ireland to the first
and favored Ramsey Barton. And they had kept it evermore. They
fought for it and married for it and schemed for it. And there was
always a male Barton to follow generation after generation,
century after century. Rockbarton Hall stood steadfast on its hillock
and looked out on prime land and cultivated fields, on estate walls

and beech and elm and chestnut.

That day, seven years ago, he saw it clearly in three parts. First the house, rebuilt over the years and finally a brilliant example of the brilliant architect Palladin. It stood on the high place, on a natural incline and managed to look as if it had been raised there artificially. All round the slope of the incline were stepped, gray slabs of limestone topped with ornate urns of plasterwork. The front, like an entrance to a Doric temple, and the later Georgian windows made an architectural joke of the great but austere Palladin. But it was barely noticeable and every other feature, too, was rendered to a minor placing, for the Virginia Creeper, burning and burnished with fall hues, set it afire, as if it were molten ore, like the sunset playing its rays on a great bronze orb on a distant hill. It sunk into his mind and stayed there.

So did the other pieces of the image. If one visualized the house as the apex of an equilateral triangle and followed the line down the left side, the chestnut tree was where the next angle would be. A spreading chestnut tree, like the house, afire in the hue of fall. Beneath it, like the spokes of a wheel, the horses stood. They stood, head to the great trunk, a dozen or more, glistening, shimmering in light mahogany coats, like the fruits of the tree itself when first opened. The horses snorted in staccato bursts, they flicked their tails, they stamped the bare earth. They created a picture of languid, lazy, wealth-filled autumn days. At the other side, completing the triangle, was the stream and the miniature waterfall and the rustic bridge, and a little beyond, the still pond covered in lily pads and hung with flowering rushes. And a wooden gazebo.

"Rockbarton," Cronin said. "My ticket to Perth." He said so almost every morning as they came through the ornate gates from the road. Cronin was twenty-one, short, stocky, handsome in a swarthy gypsy sort of way. Given the physical difference, he resembled a young version of Clark Gable. Perhaps Cronin thought so too and tried to cultivate it. There was no modern precedent in Cronin's kingdom of comparison for the penciled line moustache he wore. Most of the time Lacy was repelled by Cronin. He had read somewhere that Boswell had described somebody as not couth. That little phrase suited Cronin well. His arrogance was invariably abrasive. He had self-confidence that bordered on the egotistical. And his conversation was laced with crude vulgarities and sexual innuendo. There were times when Lacy inwardly flinched at some of the things Cronin said or described. But it was strange, Lacy thought, how Cronin could occupy the opposing ends of a divergent scale. There were times, too, when Cronin impressed him. Times when he made him envious.

Cronin was going to Australia. Lacy, in the fall, would be entering his second year in the Crawford Institute of Technology. Cronin believed he was going to the land of bountiful opportunity. Lacy knew for certain that he was heading back to his private barren hell. He hated it at Crawford. Hated the stupid macho vulgarity, the heavy emphasis on field sports. He saw it as a many peopled Cronin. He hated the course, too, and knew his old man had talked him into the wrong choice. He should have gone for arts or journalism. Perhaps if he had been able to even partially fund his education he might have been able to influence the decision. But that remained to be seen. His father was a strong-willed man. It was those divergent but twin motivations that brought Cronin and Lacy together in the summer of nineteen eighty-two. That, plus the opportunity that was Rockbarton. It was up for sale. An old photograph bedecked one full page in *Field and Country*. It looked out from the windows of real estate offices in London's stockbroker belt. The picture lied. Rockbarton had fallen on hard times over the past twelve years. All the good horses had been sold. The spreading chestnut was uprooted in a storm. There was no male heir to fight and scheme for the estate's survival. In three hundred years of male dominance, Emma Barton, a woman, young and delicate was the last of the line.

"Don't be acting the fool now," Cronin said as the car coughed down the potholed avenue. "There's five more weeks of work here if we play it right. String it out."

Cronin was an out-of-work electrician. Some smart-assed dude in a check jacket and cavalry twill pants had called at the house and offered him a job on the lump. Three hundred pounds to repair some faulty wiring in Rockbarton and string a few new cables.

Cronin took it, though he knew the smart-assed auctioneer would make as much as he for simply stopping at his home. "Beggars can't be choosers," Cronin said philosophically. That was five weeks ago; he was still working at Rockbarton. He had even managed to bring Lacy in. There was five percent commission there. Easiest money you'll ever make, Lacy thought as Cronin fought the steering wheel. Most of the time he just hung around, holding a ladder, bringing a toolbox. Cronin had developed into being general factotum. He was painter, carpenter, brick layer. And getting a week's wages—his passage to Perth.

Lacy was happy, sometimes exhilarated. Jasper Barton was a world apart, Emma a porcelain miracle of smiles and blushes and pretty moving hands. Only now was she beginning to move in his peripheral vision and he in hers. They were soul mates and it seemed that the groping, awkward auras of silence which surrounded them both were, at last, being pierced with little straining antennae of probing and halting exploration. In Lacy's mind Emma was beautiful. He had seen her once, long ago. Long ago, all of seven years, when she fed the ducks in the still pond and he watched in rapt wonder from the far bank of the Deel. He had seen her representation once more in the interval of years. He and his mother had gone to Goodwin's glassware store in Limerick. His mother wanted a present for her sister who was returning to America after a short visit to the original homestead. There was a music box with a figurine of a young teenager who pirouetted as she went round and round in time to the music. A figurine of Dresden. Wondrous delicacy, her dress a filigree of lace with a rounded hem. Apple tints in her cheeks and barely perceptible lights in her corn-colored hair. Like a star in some far distant galaxy, now and then appearing and re-appearing as in tiny pinpricks of blinding light. Lacy had spoken no more than a dozen words to Emma. Once, the first week, she smiled a thank you when he opened the stable door for her. Once they came to the pathway leading to the hothouse together and she asked him if he liked it at Crawford. And once when she brought a tin of paint from the shed and their fingers met when she handed it to him. Cronin mocked him. He made a lewd sign with his bunched fingers whenever Emma appeared in their vision. He whistled at her. Lacy felt it raise the hackles of his neck. It was a primitive primordial sound redolent of bestial rawness. Like the mating call of a rancid puck goat on a rocky promontory.

"You're like some lovesick twit," Cronin said. "Suppose you think that she's all sweetness and beauty and butter wouldn't melt in her mouth. God love you, Lacy. They're all the same in the dark."

Lacy couldn't argue with him. He'd present a reasonable logical case and Cronin would stomp all over it. Not that he ever attacked the logic and the reason. Instead he went after the words and the sentiment and when Lacy got mad Cronin would say things like: "Will you look at the head of him. Like a turkey cock. You're all reddened up today, Mr. Turkey Cock. The hen must be giving you a bad time."

For days after some event like that Lacy despised him with a terrible anger that seemed to lift the roof of his head. Cronin obviously recognized it and stayed clear. Lacy would have liked to reach out and tear the smile from his face. But when it came to driving home or stopping for a drink in Anty Ryan's, Cronin would be all solid and sensible and pragmatic. He'd say, "We work well together, Lacy. Look. Come to Perth when you're qualified. Let me know. I'll have a job waiting for you. We get on."

If Lacy could have chosen his ideal father, his nearest representation would be Jasper Barton. He was everything. From the pointed goatee beard to the shock of gun-barrel hair. From the rose in his buttonhole to the salmon fly on the band of his tweed hat. And that was just the outward expression. Jasper was articulate, urbane, intelligent and traveled. While all round him was ruin and decay, Jasper clung to the trappings of the country squire like a zealot fastened to his ideology. He may be broke, the estate falling around his ears, but Jasper lived like the gentleman that he was. He breakfasted in his bathrobe, kidneys and mushrooms on toast. Nan lit a fire in his room while he ate and ran his bath. If it was dry, he went out wearing high-topped boots and jodphurs, jacket and cravat. When it was damp or wet, he stayed in his room or just moped about in what was left of the library. He always dressed for dinner. The view, from Lacy's perspective, highly impressed him. There wasn't a subject under the sun Jasper couldn't hold forth on. And he did it with a humorful gay articulation, words of Victorian drawing room vintage, laced with modern permissiveness. Jasper was worldly and urbane, it was in his breeding. There were three hundred years of genteel development in his present person, years of status and power and colonial superiority. Except that Jasper did not think like that and even if he did, he wouldn't dwell on it for an instant. He accepted what he was with utter understanding. He was that ultimate epitomization of superiority amid lesser beings. And he wore that knowledge with simple certainty, he didn't even have to think about it or stop to fashion an explanation.

"No wonder," Lacy used to say to himself, "no wonder simple people think such men are gods."

Nan Roche was the only surviving member in a hierarchy of servants. One morning, inexplicably, she failed to show. By midday they learned that she had gone to Dublin and wasn't coming back. Jasper took the news in his confident unflappable way. He said, "Rather odd," and returned to his book. Emma took the news badly. She cried all the afternoon. She sat alone in the wooden gazebo beside the still pond. She was still there at dinner time when Lacy and Cronin were packing up to go home and Jasper had come into the cobbled stableyard. Cronin had once said that Jasper reminded him of a character out of the "War and Peace" film. Lacy thought it was apt now.

"Say," Jasper beckoned Lacy, "something's come up. Rather silly I'm afraid. Looks like old Nan has dashed off and left us. Say, young Lacy, can I talk to you. Shan't keep you."

They stopped for a drink at Anty Ryan's. Friday was payday. The auctioneer guy with the check jacket always came by on a Friday and paid them cash.

"I wouldn't do it, Lacy," Cronin said, when Anty was out of earshot. According to Cronin she had a mouth as big as Hudson Bay.

"Why wouldn't you?"

"Because, for one thing, Jasper will never pay you the extra money. That's why I insist I only deal through the auctioneer. Jasper never pays anyone. He'll screw you. Now if it were Emma that did that I could go along."

"Knock it off, Cronin. You need a mouthwash."

"And you need a dose of commonsense. Anyway, what does he want you to do? Cook, wash, muck out the remaining nags?"

"Companionship, he said."

"You must be kidding. For whom? Him or Emma? Hey," he leered, "that may have distinct possibilities for you."

"Listen, I'm getting tired of your double meaning rubbish. Anyway, it's only for three weeks; the place will be sold by then. If not before."

"Ah." Cronin smoothed out the slop ring with the bottom of his glass. "Why not? Lacy boy. Your days of virginity are over."

Lacy swung round with a reddening face. "I told you. I'm fed up listening to your dirty talk. Emma wouldn't be seen dead with the likes of you or me. And she isn't like that."

Cronin blew air loudly through his nostrils. It was his manifestation of cynicism.

"You must be kidding. She's just like all the rest. Bet you I could get off with her."

"You could. In the same way as you'd get off with Queen Elizabeth."

"You can make fun." Cronin shook his head from side to side in mock hurt. "Now if you had twenty pounds to spare, I'd have a bet with you. You'd have to give me odds, of course."

"Listen, Cronin, if I had twenty pounds I would'nt bet. It would be sinful. Like taking money from a child. You'd have two chances with the likes of Emma. None and shag all."

"Hey, that's a good one," Cronin said. "Ah well," he bobbed his head rapidly as if talking to himself, "maybe I'll do it for nothing. C'mon let's hit the road. I've a hot date with a bird from Athea."

It was raining. Outside the window full ripe raindrops plopped on the leaves of the Virginia Creeper like the sound of trout at dusk long ago. The roof leaked. Around the polished floor the containers were well placed. Pots, pans, copper and brass, like antique navigational instruments on a ship's deck. Plop. Plop. The rain struck the big leaves of the creeper and washed away the soil at the base of the wall. The rain drops hit the containers on the floor, sharper, with more precise sounds like the larger fish in faster waters. Now and then a new drop would burst on the floor. Emma would leave her position beside her father's chair and go gleefully to find another pot or pan. They both laughed, Emma and Jasper. It was really a parlor game. Finding the most unlikely container, like a chamber pot or an earthenware crock. Or guessing where the next drop would hit and drawing a circle around it with chalk and putting their initials inside the circle. Before she went to bed, Emma made the tally and declared a winner.

Lacy tried to imagine the room. He had a faint vision of it for his mother came here as a young woman to collect her wages. She worked in the harvest fields. She remembered Jasper behind a walnut writing desk, counting out the money in silver. The walnut desk was gone now, but its impression could still be seen on the floor. The great ebony and marble fireplace was gone too. The gutted surround crudely filled with unpainted cement blocks. A few portraits on the walls, sections of paneling fixed awry and some free-standing. It was all over the house, the testimony of decay and new poverty creeping like a fungus along the corridor, from room to room. Once, in harvest, they held a ball in this room. They took punch in the Great Hall, they climbed the stairs and looked through the railings at the cream of society dancing to Strauss. A phrase came into Lacy's mind. That kind of thing happened so often to him. Bits of poetry, rhyming couplets, lines from the classical writers. It must be the academic in him, the latent journalist. *Sic transit gloria mundi.*

It rained for days. Rain drops plopped. Chalk circles were drawn and erased. Jasper sat in his leather-covered armchair with the stuffing coming through the upholstered armrest. "Like a burst sausage," Cronin said when Lacy described it. Jasper, wearing evening wear, Emma haunched beside the chair; Jasper, with arms folded around his knee, spinning his web of urbanity. His school days in Sandhurst, his commission with the Irish Guards, war stories from North Africa and Monte Casino. In the room next door which had been exclusively his (he called it the War Room), he had set up the collection when he was invalided out. On an easel, placed in the alcove of a great bay window, Jasper had plotted the progress of the war. When the Allies landed at Normandy, Jasper announced at the breakfast table that the war was as good as over. The easel was still in the window bay forty years later, the Allied position frozen on a piece of cardboard now as weathered as vellum. Juno, Sword, Omaha. You could smell the heat in the room. Logs blazed in the ruined fireplace, the French polish softened on the furniture. Sparks flew from the logs and left burn marks beyond the protection of the brass fender. It was like a miniature battlefield, cratered and shelled.

Between the time after dinner and when he slept in the chair, Jasper drank most of a bottle of Bushmills whiskey. He was always in near coma by the time the grandfather clock struck the half-hour before midnight. Emma and Lacy would lift him between them and drag him to the bedroom next along the corridor. They just laid him on the bed. Sometime in the small hours of the morning he would wake and remove his dinner clothes. Before he fell into half-coma, he always signaled: he exhaled loudly, his lips made a series of smacking noises and his head drooped.

Once when Lacy rose to bring him to bed, Emma beckoned Lacy to sit and came and sat on the arm of his chair. She traced her finger along his jawline and curled the strand of his hair that fell over his forehead. So sudden, so wonderful! Lacy's breath froze and the blood rushed to his face. It lasted only for moments. When Lacy lifted his eyes, she was looking at him with deep searching discovery. As if his face were a territory on a world atlas and she was plotting a route across it. His lifting eyes seemed to break the mood. She smiled, placed her finger on his lips. Then she went and took the arm of her stupefied father. They dragged him across the bare floor. They laughed at the way his feet collided with the con-tainers and smudged the chalk circles. They laid him snoring on top of the coverlet. Emma backed out of the room and a little way down the corridor. The look of intense exploration had returned to her face. The lock snapped loudly as she closed the door of her bedroom.

"Young Lacy," Jasper said at breakfast, "how will you live your life?" He was in his dressing gown, searching for kidneys and mushrooms in a barren thermidor.

"Get a job, I suppose," Lacy said. "There must be someone out there who wants a mechanical engineer."

"Wouldn't you rather be something else?"

"I don't understand."

"Like an architect or a journalist. Preferably a journalist." Jasper turned and smiled, holding an empty toast rack. "Emma told me. I find it, well, rather intriguing. That bit about the journalist."

"You do?"

"Oh. Yes, rather. You see that should have been my profession. I was rather good at it, if I may say so. I did some drafts for the *Telegraph* and they were rather taken. Based on my journal. I always kept a journal, you know."

"I never saw the journal," Emma said.

"Oh. Rather nondescript, I'm afraid. It's in one of the drawers someplace. Remember, I came across it, ah when was Philip here?"

"Philip," Emma said for Lacy's benefit, "Philip was an old crony from the Sandhurst days. Father, that was five years ago."

"Quite. That long. Good Lord. Anyway, young Lacy, I only bring it up for the sake of the moral."

"The moral, Mr. Barton?"

"Yes, young Lacy. It's your life. We only get one crack at it. Do what you want to do. That's Emma's motto, isn't that right, young woman?"

Emma looked at him with a sideways glance. Lacy saw his mother do that, too, when she wanted to place a strange sound or puzzle something out.

"I'm not quite sure, Father."

"Of course you are. How many times have we talked about it? Be what you want, be steadfast in your pursuit, be footloose and fancy free. That's it, a free agent."

"Like mother was?"

Jasper sat. He stretched his long legs and pulled his body down as if he were a single rigid unit fastened to the seat.

"In a way, yes. I envied the old girl."

"Nice, kind, gentle words you use, Father. Are you especially benign today?"

Jasper held his hands over his head and cracked his knuckles.

"That was our Tony," he said. Knuckle on his middle finger was refusing to obey.

"Antonia was my mother," Emma said, again for Lacy's benefit. "Or should I say, Father, she gave birth to me. You see, Lacy, Father married her for money. Antonia Beatrice Wyndham. She had an awful lot of it in trust. And when her old man saw the state of Rockbarton and understood my father's intent, he froze the trust. I was five when the honorable Antonia walked out on us. Just went away. Without a good-bye. Bitch. I hardly think she's a good model to found my life on, eh Father?"

Jasper slid lower in the chair. A sunbeam built a column of light horizontally across the room. A myriad of dust particles were locked in the column, spinning and turning and falling. The beam ended on Jasper's face. Lacy could see the ravages in great detail, as if Jasper's features were under a microscope lens. His eyes were bloodshot, skin gray. His neck was like a pattern of woven rattan. He spread his hands.

"Don't think you do the old girl justice, Emma. Up and go. It's not a bad philosophy. Make no ties, no binding relationships, don't get strapped down. Remember that, young Lacy. I was too old when I discovered that."

Once Lacy had heard his father talk about the fish pond. He talked about it to his neighbors with the quiet emphasis of near incredulity. An ancestor named Reuben Barton had created the fish pond. There was a portrait of him in the library, black visaged, deep eyes, small slit for a mouth without a cupid's bow. As mad as a March hare, the folklore said he was. Wild, unpredictable, eccentric. He would throw off his clothes and dance, naked except for his high boots, on the dining room table. And do it at the harvest banquet when the courtyard and stairs and landing were filled with his wide-eyed tenantry. Reuben made the fish pond. He ran a spur from the River Deel, across three fields of limestone. And on late summer evenings he sat and watched the trout rise and shot them with a sixteen bore Smith and Wesson. Reuben was mad. Mad, and unpredictable and cruel.

All that was left of the wooden gazebo were the floor tiles. They had been cut and hewn from the trunk of an oak tree. It was evening and a frog croaked beneath a lily pad. Emma sat on a blackened oak tile and dangled her feet in the lily pond. The water was stagnant and when the breeze lifted the air held the smell of vegetable putrefaction.

"I heard that Reuben was mad," Lacy said.

Lacy had his pants pulled up beyond his knees. Emma traced a line of glistening wet along his calf. She did it with her big toe. She laughed and drew her foot away.

"People said he was mad. But he wasn't."

"As mad as a March hare, my father said."

"People said that because they didn't understand. In his time Reuben had the best crop of yearlings ever to come out of Rockbarton. He was the most successful of all Rockbarton masters. He had great ambition and great vitality. People like him get bored easily."

She jumped up and the young breeze lifted the cotton dress high above her thighs. Lacy shot his eyes away.

"He built that fish pond," he said. It was an accusation, the way the words came out. "He built it, a useless vain folly when the country was going through a famine. People were dying in the thousands. Women and little children."

She came to him and put her finger against his lips.

"You sound like Cronin! And others that I have heard. They all have one solution. Pull us all down to the same level. Tell me, Lacy," (she still kept her fingers pressed in a silent gesture of paradox) "what good would it have done if Reuben hadn't built his pond? Would it have stopped the famine?"

She took his hand and led him to where the natural spring came out of the rock and tumbled down in a miniature waterfall. Directly below the fall, the water had eroded a small pool, dark and cold against the bed of peat and decayed matter. She drew her fingers along the surface and knelt to watch the ripple widening and disappearing.

"Does your father really believe that?" Lacy asked. "About being footloose and fancy free? Like your mother was, without ties or roots?"

She made a crude boat from a lily pad and put it in the pool. She churned the water and watched the boat rock and toss in the miniature storm.

"One is never sure about the things my father says. He's inclined to exaggerate, especially as night wears on. But I think I understand what he was trying to tell us."

She walked a few steps away, down to the edge of the stagnant pond. Over the years it had overgrown. You could still make out the original perimeter rising like a saucer above the small depression in the middle. All that was now left.

"When I was young they caught the last fish. I was seven. Nan brought me down to the pantry to show me. It was a bream. They argued about it for days. How did the bream get in? Reuben had stocked it with rainbow trout."

"I'm not sure if your father likes me," Lacy said.

"It's not that he doesn't like you," Emma smiled. She pulled a reed from the edge to steer the makeshift boat from the overhang of peat. "He thinks that we're attracted to each other. And he's afraid of that. And he thinks you're too intent, too sensitive, too serious for your years. And he thinks that such young men can exert too much influence over impressionable sheltered girls like me."

She hadn't looked at him. All the time she was maneuvering the boat with the reed, poking it into dark corners under the overhang, probing it out again. Lacy could feel his neck warming, the beginning of embarrassment, a tentacle of unease, like the reed she held in her hand, probed the growing emotion in his soul and laid an icy ring around the outer edges of it.

"I'm very attracted to you, Lacy. I'm attracted to you for the very things my father fears. And if I know that, what I feel will grow and change and develop into something more serious."

"Like what?"

"You shouldn't ask me. For then you'll have got me to say the word and I don't think that's fair."

"I'll say it if you want."

She impaled the reed into the soft peat and watched it vibrate.

"I'll say the word if you like."

She closed her eyes as if she already heard the words and the sound was musical and honeyed. And she came beside him and pressed his lips closed.

"Don't say it. You see, Lacy, my father is right. And please, please, don't say anything. Look at it from his view for a moment. I'm all he's got. The only mealticket he has. I have to look after him and provide. And right now there's a very serious young man beginning to become a threat to that."

"And you, Emma, do you see me as that too?"

Far away a corncrake cried. Lacy heard it distinctly and abstracted the significance of it. The corncrake was almost extinct. Mostly because of new farming methods that desecrated it's natural cover. And yet, here in Rockbarton it lived. Amid the decay and the hopelessness and the ruin, the bird survived. Mother Nature plays strange tricks on all those who people her earth.

"Did you hear the corncrake, Lacy?" Her eyes lighted then suddenly dulled. "If Nan were here she'd be delighted. I wonder did Father hear?"

"Emma, listen. What do you think? I asked you."

"Sch. Sch. Maybe we'll hear it again."

They listened in the still of the evening. A horse whinnied, the rook set up a sudden cacophony in the tall trees beyond the stables. Across many fields a man called angrily to his dog. It was all over. Whatever it was before the corncrake shrilled, whatever the mood held or was leading to, was now all shattered and gone. Lacy looked at his feet as if he might see the broken pieces there.

"Lacy, I'm thirsty. I'd love a drink of water from the spring."

He cupped his hands together and squeezed them tightly. When he lifted them from the tiny pool, the water spilled out through the cracks of his fingers. She put her face in the container of his hands and first drank. Then she kissed his fingers and lifting her wetted lips with glistening drops, she kissed him full on the mouth. His mind spun and in that spinning moment he thought he heard the corncrake again.

They walked shoulder to shoulder along the gravel path overhung with rank toppling grasses. They came into the sun dappled glade where the light gathered, before it lost itself in the dark tunnel of trees beyond. They came out onto the cobbled courtyard and heard her father call from his room on the second floor.

"You know something?" she said.

Lacy shook his head.

"If I never hear the corncrake again, I will never forget when I last heard it. She ran across the cobblestones. He ran after and she waited at the pillar of the great carved stairway.

"I asked you a question."

"You should see yourself, Lacy. So intent and serious. You know what I think, Lacy? I wish you were Cronin. No. No. Not that, but I wish some parts of you were Cronin."

He slept in a room that had been painted an eggshell blue. Once it was Daphne's room. She was Jasper's sister and she had died of pulmonary tuberculosis a week before her twenty-second birthday. It was the best kept room in the house, mainly because Jasper's mother had closed it up when Daphne died and it had the effect of preserving it. He and Emma had taken off the covers from the furniture, put the brassbound bed together again and removed the yellowing paper from the pictures. The memory of sad, dead Daphne permeated the room. She looked out at Lacy from the portrait above the foot of the bed. She stood beside a horse, mousy and frail and non-descript. Nothing, the riding clothes she wore, the silver topped riding crop, the velvet hat, nothing added any substance to the picture of her. It seemed that if the horse suddenly lifted it's head the movement would lift Daphne off her feet. The air in the room was musty and dry and brittle. Lacy slept badly. Even here the roof leaked and the drops plopped and exploded on the polished floor boards. And Daphne's sick tubercular ghost tormented his imagination. He thought she was haunting his dreams when the door creaked open and a frail, nightgown-clad figure came to his bed. There was a single shaft of light where the moon slid through the branches of an ancient tree. The figure was caught in the light. Billowing and ethereal and willowy. But the light exposed Emma's face, the smile around the corners of her mouth, the finger of silence pressed to her lips. She drew back the covers and slid in beside him. She propped the pillow against the brass headrest and lit two cigarettes. In the darkness, when they inhaled, a soft warm glow, the color of an autumn leaf, crept up the wainscoting. It came and went like the afterglow of a sunken sun on a far, far horizon. Before the cigarette was finished she stubbed it out on the floorboards and slid under the blankets.

"Lacy," she said in a soft, muffled voice, "I place my trust in you."

His heart thumped. He heard the old clock in the hall with the flaking veneer strike quarter-hour, and hour, and half-hour. His heart thumped. She stirred and moved and rolled against him. What did she mean when she said I place my trust in you? God. Lacy, you fool, if Cronin knew about this you'd be the laughing stock of the land. He finally slept as he was, his back against the brass rest, his neck warming the cold metal. In the morning when he woke she was gone. Then he knew he had dreamt her coming into his bed. He was certain it was a dream until he saw the stubbed out cigarette butt on the floorboards.

In the evening after there was great excitement. Nan was back. A young boy had cycled in from the road and told Jasper that Nan was in Ardagh waiting for a lift to Rockbarton. Jasper sent Cronin in the car to fetch her. He only went, he said, because he needed felt nails for the roof of the lean-to against the barn. Lacy heard Emma shouting when the car came back from Ardagh. It was the first he had seen of her all morning. She was racing across the cobbled courtyard to meet old Nan. She was wearing a cotton print dress that billowed when she ran and exposed her thighs. Lacy closed his eyes and shut out the scene. But he heard the wolf whistle that Cronin made as he lifted Nan's things from the boot.

In the late evening, as Lacy rubbed down the horse in the stable, Emma came as far as the stable door. She stood for a moment, as if shocked, then she attempted a smile and went back into the house. A few minutes later Jasper came out. It was all right now he said. Nan was back. They wouldn't be needing him anymore at night. He never mentioned anything about the extra money, and Lacy never spoke with Emma again.

Less than a week after Nan came back the estate agent came out to Cronin's house. The work was winding down; they had done enough to satisfy the foreign estate agent. And the few things that were left Cronin could do on his own. It was the end of Lacy's world. The final act that brought the curtain down on the shattered fragments that were his soul and his heart. He could never find the words to explain it to anyone, not even to himself and most of all not to Emma. For Lacy, the gauche adolescent, the confused and the halting, the trusting and the maimed, was in love. The shyness and the confusion would never allow the word to come through so he found a way to gather all those things in his mind and to stow them unexpressed. It was so apt for his condition, a finger pressed gently against his lips. A silent token of the confused emotion that tumbled about in his soul. It was that one simple gesture that bespoke all the other things they had known and shared—words, unspoken sentiment, a kiss full on his lips, her mouth drinking from his cupped hands, a cigarette glowing in the darkness of Daphne's bedroom. And when he walked the roads about his home, and when he walked alone in the darkness, he yearned for that one single expression. There was no need for words, no need for half-formed sentiment, only a finger pressed against his lips. In the end the resolve was greater than the confusion and the awkwardness. He would lay his soul at her feet.

He went in the moonlight to the place where Reuben had built his fishpond. He could smell the decaying vegetation and imagine a crude boat made from a lily pad. The moon was full, burning brightly in a cloudless sky and bathing the trees and Rockbarton chimney pots. Emma was in the gazebo. She was standing on tiptoe and her arms were about the neck of a black haired, swarthy youth. He saw then that the young man was Cronin. When Cronin laughed at something she said, she pressed her finger against his lips.

T.G. Nestor, one of a family of ten, grew up in a remote part of rural Ireland in the 1950's. He has been writing about fifteen years, mostly short stories and radio plays, usually with a rural Ireland bent. His work is best known in Ireland, Scotland and England, and his talent is gaining recognition in the USA.

"...if I were to do all that I am disposed to do and that is in my power to do, on behalf of a brother-in-law, a relation, no one would offer a word of criticism."

The Ransom

BY LEONARDO SCIASCIA

"YOUR Majesty," said Minister of State Santangelo, tapping Ferdinand lightly on the shoulder with one finger, "this is Grotte."

The king awoke with a hiccup, tried to focus his watery eyes, still heavy with sleep, upon the minister sitting opposite him and passed the back of his hand over his mouth from which ran a trickle of saliva.

"What's the matter?" he asked.

"This is the town of Grotte, Your Majesty."

Ferdinand peered out of the carriage window at a jumble of gray houses clinging to the side of a hill, roofs sprouting moss and nettles, black-clad women standing in doorways, children with startled, hungry eyes, pigs rooting among piles of rubbish.

He drew back.

"And what is the reason for my being awoken?" he asked the minister. And continued, as if addressing a third person: "Twenty-four hours without a wink of sleep, and as soon as I manage to drop off this idiot has to wake me up with the glad tidings that we are passing through Grotte!"

His underlip, which looked like a cow's kidney, trembled with vexation. He turned again to the window. A few paces from the carriage a group of silent people was forming.

"Grottoes are infested with wolves. Forward!" he shouted to the escort; then slumped back against the cushions, laughing heartily at his own wit. The minister doubled up with mirth.

They pushed on for another two miles, to Racalmuto where they found the balconies hung with silken drapes as if for the festival of Corpus Christi, the civic guard smartly drawn up and a banquet awaiting them in the town hall.

Thus was Grotte ("Le Grotte" in the documents of the time, "Li Grutti" as the people of Racalmuto still call it) deprived of the honor of receiving King Ferdinand.

Exactly one hundred years later, the train carrying Mussolini sped through the station at Grotte past crowds packed so densely on the platform that they almost overflowed onto the line itself; yet few caught even a glimpse of the bronzed, scowling face of the Duce or the sallow, smiling one of his companion, Starace.

Until only a few years ago, these two incidents continued to inspire a good deal of scorn and derision on the part of the inhabitants of Racalmuto at the expense of those of Grotte. And the latter, for their part, possessed a sizeable repertoire of mimi (comic playlets in mime after the style of Francesco Lanza, the collector and arranger of a series of such pieces and by whom they were christened mimi) which burlesqued the defects of the inhabitants of Racalmuto.

When Grotte met Racalmuto on the football field, the recitation of these historical incidents and of the mimi, the hurling of insult and invective, continued until five minutes before the whistle—at which point verbal abuse was replaced by physical assault, by punches, kicks and stone-throwing.

In truth, the two towns, although only separated by a couple of miles, were as different as could be. Grotte had a Protestant minority and a Socialist majority, three or four families of Jewish descent and a strong Mafia; it also had bad roads, mean houses and dreary festivals. Racalmuto staged a festival that lasted a whole week and was splendidly colorful and extravagant; the people of Grotte flocked to it in their hundreds; but for the rest of the year the town was tranquil and trouble-free, being electorally divided between two great families, having a handful of Socialists, an army of priests and a Mafia divided against itself.

Relations between the two towns were sweetened over the years and their rivalries muted not only by the march of progress but also, undoubtedly, by the frequent marriages between Grottesi and Racalmutesi; marriages which, although for the most part painstakingly arranged by intermediaries, were nevertheless usually happy.

One such marriage, which took place a few years before the demise of the Kingdom of the Two Sicilies, has become part of the folklore of both communities, not because of any element of fairytale romance, cruel parental opposition or deeds of blood, but only, perhaps, because of the beauty of a young girl, or possibly because of the events that occurred in its wake provide such a clear picture of a particular society at a particular time.

The marriage, between Don Luigi M., a well-to-do doctor of Racalmuto and a daughter of Don Raimondo G., a wealthy landowner of Grotte, had been celebrated with all the pomp expected of two such families and the life of the newlyweds was running smoothly and harmoniously in the splendid house at Racalmuto, with the husband, a full-blooded man of immense stature, full of shy attentions towards his young bride, a mere slip of a girl, when a dreadful accident occurred. In the course of an argument with one of his tenant farmers, Don Luigi lost his temper and lashed out at the man with his boot. This was, of course, an entirely legitimate way for a gentleman to resolve a dispute with a peasant, but in this case either the peasant was not endowed with the same robust constitution as Don Luigi, or maybe the kick damaged some vital organ; anyway the fact remains, according to the descendant of Don Luigi who told me the story, that the man, after staggering three times round the room, fell under a table, curled himself into a ball, and died.

The law was to be reckoned with even in those days; though

more timid, more biddable where gentlemen were concerned, a corpse was a corpse and Don Luigi faced inevitable arrest. He fled, leaving his young bride alone in the splendid house.

At the social club there was an immediate sense of outrage among the élite citizenry—not, of course, directed at poor Don Luigi. Old Don Ottavio, in his bitterness of heart, coined a phrase which achieved immediate currency and which has remained in use as an ironic adage to this day: "What a world we live in nowadays, when a gentleman can't even kick a peasant!" Everyone agreed with him: the world was indeed in a sorry state!

Don Luigi had certainly not gone very far; he might even have been in Grotte, staying with relatives or friends he could trust. But it was still inconvenient, and the thought of his young wife, alone and afraid, all frills and tenderness, lying in the big bed with its silken damask hangings, tortured him unbearably.

The good offices of influential friends werre sought in an attempt to spirit away the warrant for his arrest: the warrant which, garnished with the delicate butterfly-like emblem of the Bourbon lilies, the Captain of the Guard kept hanging on a nail beside his office desk. Don Luigi's father-in-law, a man of great resource and a vast circle of friends, had tried in vain for some considerable time to discover "the right string to pull" when, by a stroke of sheer good luck, it fell into his hands one December evening when he was sitting in his dressing gown by the fireside, reading *Il Monitore* while his daughter Concettina worked away at her embroidery, in coral beads and gold thread, of a picture of the Infant Jesus totally naked except for a band from which hung, dangling between the crooked baby legs, a little bell. The original from which Concettina was copying was a devotional image given to her by her aunt who was a nun. Don Raimondo considered the little bell to be in grossly bad taste but kept his counsel, fearing to cast doubt both upon the innocence of the nuns, who held the image in veneration, and upon that of his daughter who was copying the picture with such loving attention. But the thought of that little bell gnawed at him as he read his paper and he determined to speak to his wife about it and ask her to persuade Concettina to relinquish the embroidery.

Thus, when his thoughts were interrupted by a furious knocking at the front door, the first words that came to his lips as he went to open it were: "Put that little bell out of sight!" And when Concettina failed to grasp his meaning, he cried: "That thingummy-bob...the Infant Jesus," fearing that the visitor, whoever he was, might make mischief on the subject of Concettina's purity.

The visitor was a personage of some importance, no less than Don Nicola Cirino, jurist and poet, Procurator General of Palermo. His carriage had broken down at the gates of Grotte, in a night of bitter cold and howling wind, and, unable to continue his journey, he had been accompanied to Don Raimondo's house, the best in town.

Don Nicola was a man of about sixty, with gray hair and a gray beard, somewhat wizened and with a general air of decrepitude; but his eyes were piercing and lively, contrasting curiously with the impression of bone-weariness and imminent collapse.

Don Raimondo, whose reactions were always swift, directed a prayer of thanksgiving to the Almighty for having sent a night such as this, positioned a stone on the road and arranged for the coachman to suffer a moment's distraction. For these were the circumstances, as Don Nicola explained while apologizing for the inconvenience to which he was putting the household, which had caused the accident.

Don Raimondo assured him that far from being an inconvenience, this was an honor, a pleasure...

Concettina had put away her embroidery. Don Raimondo now presented her to Don Nicola and, in her shyness, she blushed the color of a ripe peach. Her beauty was extraordinary: a graceful figure, hair the color of caramel and a face that combined a timid sweetness with irrepressible gaiety, the gaiety that can see the comic side of everything, including trouble. Don Nicola was moved to thoughts—in verse—of a branch of wild roses, of oranges cradled in green foliage beneath the snow, of the morning star...And, still in the poetry which came so easily to him when he was inspired by beauty, he compared his heart to a volcano erupting with molten streams of passion. Since he already knew all about the warrant issued for the arrest of Don Raimondo's son-in-law, all the codices, Pandects, indictments and sentences lay from that moment like votary offerings at the feet of a sixteen-old girl.

It was a very pleasant evening. The improvised supper turned out splendidly. Seals bearing the imprint of that unpropitious year 1848 were broken but the wine in their bottles proved to be excellent. On top of that, the imprint of 1848 served as a pretext for the introduction of topics upon which Don Nicola and Don Raimondo held identical opinions. They drank each other's health. Don Nicola proposed toasts in verse to the mistress of the house, who, in her hastily-donned satin, had assumed the splendor of a rose in full bloom, and to Concettina. Then, in response to requests from Don Raimondo, the signora and, shyly, from Concettina, he recited a poem he had written about Torquato Tasso. When he arrived at the lines:

> Tho' darkling pleasures sweetened bitter days
> For that great, grieving soul, yet was his life
> So trammell'd and oppress'd that from his heart
> All hope, alas! had fled, and torment reigned
> To gnaw and burn unceasingly; his sighs
> Were those of one who almost feeds on grief.
> If he might be consoled by loving tears,
> Divine compassion, tenderness of heart,
> Eleonora...

he fastened upon Concettina the languishing gaze of a dying man, and, leaning over the table towards her, pronounced the name "Eleonora" in a way that left no doubt but that he meant "Concettina;" this was not lost upon Don Raimondo and his wife, who exchanged worried glances.

After complimenting the poet, Don Raimondo skillfully edged the conversation round to the subject of the misfortune suffered by another daughter of his, whose husband, under threat of arrest, had been forced to flee God knows where, leaving the girl, only a few months after her wedding, all alone; and all because of a peasant having been kicked...At this rate, society was in a fair way of being stood on its head...Yes, the law had to be obeyed; but one foolish kick in a moment of temper...

Don Nicola seemed to have withdrawn into some world of his own; he watched Concettina and said nothing. He was weighing up the pros and cons of a scheme he had in mind; he had already decided to chance his arm, but was still undecided as to whether he should do so at once or wait until morning.

"Can we have a word in private?" he asked suddenly, the decision made.

Mother and daughter arose in some slight confusion, and, at a nod from Don Raimondo, left the room.

Swirling the wine around the bottom of his glass, Don Nicola said with a smile, "Don Raimondo, would you like to have your son-in-law back with you in time for Christmas?"

"Need you ask?" said Don Raimondo, thinking: With a man in his position, this could cost me a fortune.

Neither spoke for a few moments.

"Contrary to what you're thinking, I'm not talking about money," said Don Nicola, "but about something infinitely more valuable, something which is, to both you and me, not only precious but priceless. Can you not guess?"

"St. Anthony Abbot!" exclaimed Don Raimondo, who invariably invoked the patron saint of the town in moments of crisis. He had indeed guessed, and the effect was cataclysmic, making, for the moment, all thought impossible.

"I see I have shocked you, and appreciate the reasons for such a reaction. I assure you that a refusal would not surprise me in the least, and should that happen, this sociable evening that we have spent would still remain a very pleasant memory. But I'm sure you understand things; given my position, if I were to do all that I am disposed to do and that is in my power to do, on behalf of a brother-in-law, a relation, no one would offer a word of criticism. People would merely say: 'He saved his brother-in-law from prison, anyone would do the same.' But for a complete stranger..."

"You're right," said Don Raimondo.

"I'm glad you understand. So give it some thought, discuss it with your wife, and with your daughter...And let me know your decision tomorrow before I leave. And now we won't mention the subject again until tomorrow."

Don Raimondo summoned the maid and sent her to inform the ladies that they might return. His wife searched his face anxiously, trying to read his thoughts. They drank cordial and Concettina played devotional songs and romances at the piano while Don Nicola gazed at her besottedly, leaning so low over the instrument that his head seemed about to drop on to the keyboard and roll into Concettina's lap.

When the clock chimed midnight, Don Nicola, to the great relief of his hosts, finally decided to retire for the night. He wished them all a good night with many a flowery speech and was barely out of the room before the signora turned upon Don Raimondo. "What did he want?" she asked with avid anxiety.

Without satisfying his wife's curiosity, Don Raimondo turned to Concettina and asked her if she loved her sister. Concettina did indeed. More questions and more answers followed, forming a kind of domestic catechism beween father and daughter, Concettina never straying once from a purely orthodox line, from what was expected of her and from the principles of self-sacrifice for which her whole upbringing had so rigidly, yet so tenderly, prepared her.

Finally, having assured himself that Concettina was prepared to help her sister no matter what the cost to herself, Don Raimondo told her that Don Luigi's return to his wife, his lands and his patients, and his exculpation in the eyes of the law, all turned upon her marriage to Don Nicola.

Concettina began to laugh, and laugh, and laugh; then the laughter turned into a convulsive, desperate storm of tears. But when her mother, too, began to weep and even Don Raimondo failed to restrain a trembling tear, she calmed down and between the tears said yes, she would marry Don Nicola.

As everyone was impatient that the thing should be done as quickly as possible, Don Nicola because he was consumed with passion, and Don Raimondo and the family because they wanted Don Luigi free at once, the arrangements were pushed ahead with all possible speed. For a week the house was awash with billows of lawn and crisp new linen, with bedcovers of wool and shining silk in every color of the rainbow. The word "bed," constantly recurring in such permutations as "bed-cover" and "bed-linen" ("twenty-four sets of bed-linen for the trousseau") became, in Concettina's mind, a single concrete image of almost feverish repugnance. None of this showed in her face, however, bent with such sweetness over the embroidery upon which the Infant Jesus, complete with little bell, continued to take shape. And Don Nicola regarded her ecstatically; for the old goat in love, the little bell rang out in celebration of innocence and added a touch, only a touch, of delicious obscenity.

Thus it came about that the literary work of ample bulk and fundamental importance upon which Don Nicola had been engaged, *The Institution of the Monarchy in Sicily,* remained uncompleted. Love for his child-bride distracted the distinguished lawyer-poet and then gently finished him. Concettina awoke one morning about six months after her marriage to find her husband peacefully dead beside her. He had passed away silently during the night like a candle whose flame leaps once before it gutters into darkness.

Concettina returned to her father's house a widow, and extremely rich.

Six months had not yet passed before she eloped one moonlit night, herself as palely beautiful as the moon in her black widow's weeds, with a young man from Racalmuto who, though he had said nothing, had been in love with her since before her marriage. A handsome, elegant young man of good family, but liberal and spendthrift.

Don Raimondo only forgave them on his deathbed.

I was reminded of this story, which had made a great impression upon me as a boy, when I entered the Church of St. Dominic in Palermo where Don Nicola lies buried together with all the other great Sicilians. And I was moved to write it down by one of those unforeseen promptings that can be inspired by a certain sensation, a chance encounter or a passage in a book. I had been re-reading Baudelaire and came across these lines: "Mais de toi je n'implore, ange, que tes prières, Ange plein de bonheur, de joie et de lumières!" These words, and the title of the poem in which they occur, "Reversibilité," echo somewhat ironically the catholic concept of vicarious payment which has become, in Sicily, a cardinal dogma of the agonizing religion of the family. The guilty ransomed by the innocent. In this case a girl from Grotte had paid the ransom for a man from the neighboring and hostile town of Racalmuto.

Born in Sicily, in 1921, Leonardo Sciascia is one of Italy's outstanding writers. His work covers short stories, novels, essays and plays, but he is best known for his sophisticated mysteries concerned with the complex crimes of governments. Luigi Barzini has written of him: "He is something more than one of Europe's great contemporary writers...He is also that very rare thing, a moral teacher...a poet at heart, a great novelist, and a compassionate but cruel lover of his people and his land." Mr. Sciasica now divides his time between Paris and Palermo. Avril Bardoni translated this story.

"...I restored it to its nest—with an unwilling hand
and yet with a sense of rightness that cheered
my innocent heart."

The Kingfisher:
an Ecotheological
Parable for Our Times

BY JOSEPH JOHN

THE old bridge that spanned the lagoon—and on which I was standing—had long since ceased to be a symbol of man's "conquest" of Nature. It was as though, after years of coexistence, the lagoon and the bridge—Nature and human engineering—had arrived at some sort of rapport. And I thought of a story by Kipling in which an English engineer who built a bridge across the Ganges was troubled in his dreams by the offended gods, who eventually decided to leave him alone.

From these thoughts I was awakened by the sharp hunting cry of a kingfisher scanning the waters for fish as he flew westward over the bridge. Suddenly he halted in midair, like an arrow arrested in its flight. For a moment or two he stood thus in motionless denial of the law of gravity. Then down he dropped with folded wings—down and down until, touching and yet not touching the water in a split-second maneuver of absolute deftness, he grabbed a little fish and darted eastward over my head toward a grove of coconut palms on the lagoon's east shore.

The silver sheen of the fish and the chromatic splendor of his captor lingered after they had vanished from my sight. In my mind they blended and became a power—a power that stirred my inmost being. I felt the irony of what I saw—of beauty destroying beauty, life killing life. I felt the cruelty of the universal law which decrees that no living creature shall subsist without preying on its fellow-creatures. I thought of the Khmer civilization that flourished on the sale of kingfisher feathers. I thought, too, of the avatar of Vishnu in the form of a fish. And I had glimpses of a fantastic web of dark meanings woven of conflict and harmony.

For a moment the bridge seemed an arch of sorrow athwart all existence. But the lagoon smiled in calm contentment. And the palms were praying.

Yet the image of the kingfisher, with the fish helpless in his beak, haunted my mind. My thoughts went back to the days of my childhood when I used to dream of having little birds to play with. And I remembered how I once picked up an unfledged kingfisher from its nest and how, moved by its plaintive cries, I restored it to its nest—with an unwilling hand and yet with a sense of rightness that cheered my innocent heart.

"What may have become of that fledgling?" I asked myself. And in my mind I saw, with dismay, an adult kingfisher—a full-fledged predator—scouring lakes and streams for prey. And my thoughts took on a somber coloring from a crimson sun that stood on the western wave—beyond the lagoon, beyond the white stretch of sand between the lagoon and the sea, beyond the merchant vessel that steamed northward on its solitary course.

That night, as I slept, this kingfisher of my childhood visited me in my dream. Not as the helpless fledgling I had restored to its nest, but as the full-grown kingfisher that had become a predator. Impulsively, I stretched out my hand to catch him and wring his neck. Suddenly, a voice thundered within me that said, "Desist!" My whole being shook as the dire history of man's cruelty to his non-human fellow-creatures unrolled within me in a flash. Guilty and ashamed, I withdrew my punitive hand.

And now, flanked by the bright dreams and sable visions of all my forebears—human and pre-human—my soul emerged, serene amidst the tumults of my mind. There it stood, a spark of the primordial sun of Being whose spirit dwells within and beyond the spaceless bounds of Hiranyagarbha, the Cosmic Womb. There it stood, looking tenderly at the kingfisher. A blessedness beyond all human speech was between the twain; I could hardly tell one from the other. And I saw myriad living forms lose themselves in that blessedness in a mysterious merging of identities. And my soul now was unto itself a song of songs; a paean to the Cross of universal convergence, a canticle to the all-creating, all-conserving, all-redeeming Christ of the Cosmos.

 *Joseph John's short stories, articles, poems and book reviews appear in journals in Jordan, USA, India and Germany. He was born in Kerala and received his Ph.D. in English literature from Marquette University, Milwaukee. Dr. John teaches on the university level in Jordan. He has also taught in Sri Lanka, Singapore, India and Ethiopia. He translated this story from his original work written in Malayalam.*

"The vaunted spirit was to be known by him
only through the regimen which she
had imposed on their lives."

People of Consequence

BY INES TACCAD-CAMMAYO

CAMUS and his wife secretly prided themselves in being, of all the residents in their barrio, the only ones who had really known and lived with people of consequence.

When he was a young man, Camus had been the houseboy of a German hacendero. The German who was a bachelor had often told Camus that his punishments were for his own good because he must learn to shed his indolent and clumsy ways if he ever hoped to amount to anything. Unfortunately, before he could learn more from his stern master, his father wrote to say that he must come home right away because his betrothed was waiting. The German had mouthed unintelligible, guttural curses which Camus listened to with mixed feelings of shame and pleasure because it meant that he was wanted and needed after all. But in the end, the German sent him off with a *de hilo cerrada* suit, a heavy pair of boots capacious enough to let him wiggle his gnarled toes in, and two months extra pay which came in handy for the wedding celebration. That was twenty-five years ago, shortly before the war, and although Camus had all intentions to see the German off when he left for his country, the expense and the effort turned out to be, at the last minute, discouraging. In the meantime, Camus and his wife were themselves becoming people of consequence.

They now owned the best house in the barrio which, with other lakeside villages, lay at the base of a high cliff which the people called Munting Azul because a perpetual haze clung to its summit. To reach the summit, one must climb the steep and circuitous steps that many years ago, the men, Camus among them, had hacked out of the thick underbrush that covered the entire face of the cliff, and then cemented in places where the downrushing water in rainy seasons was wont to wash away.

One could also leave the village by crossing the lake westward. The upward climb was the quicker route but was difficult for the old and the weak. Once the high embankment was reached, Munting Azul leveled off into fields, and three kilometers away was the town of Cuenco.

The town was bypassed by the national highway but jeepneys and a couple of minibuses shuttled to and from the larger towns, including the Capitolyo, on the descent. Cuenco was the only large town which Camus really knew although he had been to the Capitolyo occasionally. When he lived with the German, they resided in what was called the White House in the middle of a vast, treeless hacienda rimmed by the forests across the lake.

Meding, his wife, had, in her own adolescence, lived in the Capitolyo for almost four years as a servant of the Mayor's family. It was there that she learned the hard-driving manners of townfolk. It constantly amazed him how she could make idle time yield profit, and even more astonishing, how, having made profit, she held on to it. Camus, a hard worker, was at his fishing long before dawn, and later in the day, mending his nets on the pier he had built from his hut. It was his father's life he had learned, and after he came from the German's household he saw no cause and no way to change.

The first thing that Meding did was to barter, over his vehement objections, the one male carabao he owned for a puny female.

When it began to yield milk, she gathered it to make into a white curd which she moulded into banana leaf containers or boiled into sweet candy. Not one *frasco* found its way to their table. Every Sunday she would climb the steep ascent to sell her white cheese and milk sticks in Cuenco.

She gathered the occasional coconuts and mangoes from the trees behind their house and sold them, together with the harvest of fish Camus hauled in everyday. She was so undemanding, she never had to sell at a loss or to mortgage his catch, and the hard-dealing middleman who came with his tempting offers by-passed their house with great aloofness.

Meding even opened a postal savings account and once in a while she showed him the figures. As the sum increased he felt he knew her less and less. Long before she began the feverish phase of acquiring possessions, when they sat down to their frugal meal he felt that, perhaps they could afford something more appetizing. A look at Meding's face bent over her plate, contented in determined self-denial would silence him.

She astounded him most by buying crochet thread and needles. In the mornings, keeping by herself from the village women, she sat at the window of the little hut thrusting away at her hook and thread, making beautiful patterns of lace that he believed, his heart bursting with pride, no other wife in all the lakeside barrios could make, let alone, possess her infinite patience. To his unbelieving ears, she whispered that the heavy laces were so prized that housewives in the town willingly paid for them with sacks of rice.

In time their neighbors ran to them for loans, and although she never charged usurious rates, Meding was as hard as stone when it came to collecting. If the borrower failed to pay on time, she demanded goods in payment. Her laconic and unsmiling manner defeated any jocose attempt at gaining time and even a whining plea brought only the unfeeling retort that life was just as hard for her, and that always shamed them into paying, for no one better than their neighbors knew how spartan was their life.

The first change in the quiet girl he married came one night; lying, facing each other on the slatted floor of their bedroom in the hut which was now their kitchen, she spoke of her plans, spelled each dream so grimly as to leave no doubt in Camus' mind that these were already real. Talk of a child had long since been avoided. Now she spoke of bringing in kiln-dried posts from Cuenco, a proposal wildly ostentatious and impossible, considering the steep descent from the town. She spoke of galvanized roofing, capiz windows and all the accoutrements of town houses: hardware, varnished walls, two big bedrooms, a sala so spacious it could accommodate their old hut, and carved narra furniture. When the house was finally finished—a reality of shining walls and costly gleaming windows—Camus went about apologizing for its size. "We really planned to have it much bigger, but my wife with her usual good sense wanted something more modest."

The house never wore a coat of paint, growing darker and rain-stained with every passing season. The big bedroom was never occupied except when out-of-town officials came. It contained a monstrous, carved and highly varnished bed; its snaky posts bore aloft a wooden balance that gave it unusual elegance. A three-panel mirrored aparador in the room was used by no one except their guests; so, too, a washbowl inlaid with mother of pearl which gleamed against the mahogany shadows of the room.

One day Meding said, "The young men are going up to the Capitolyo next week. It would be a good time for you to go with them." After a long pause, she added, "They invite you every year but you have gone only once. You could visit with the Superintendente this time."

At an earlier fiesta, when Camus arrived at the Inspector's house, the official was already taken up with his other visitors. The señora did not know him. She must have also been distracted at the never ending stream of visitors. With an absent-minded wave of her hand and a murmured acknowledgment, she ordered someone to unburden him of his coop of chicken and made him feel at home.

"Well, don't just stand there!" an old crone had cackled at him. "Dress the chickens!" With that she thrust a bolo into his hands. Camus was dismayed, but only for a few seconds. He spent the rest of the day cheerfully helping out in the backyard, very much needed and feeling useful as he stirred a huge carajay. He had caught a glimpse of the Inspector but the man was deep in conversation with some important-looking men. In a way, he was glad. He had stripped down to his shorts to save his *americana* from stain.

His only regret about that visit, however, was his not having been able to join in talk with the townsmen. When they came to his house, he never felt shy, telling his favorite recollections of Señor Lehmann, the German master whom many of them had heard of but never saw.

"He was a man of few words and a great reader. There was this thick book which he always read but would never let me touch. Otherwise he was extremely generous with other things. Advice. His old clothes. Sometimes money.".

As the years passed, his stories of intimacy with the German master grew, and there were times when he ventured saying that he was such the confidante of the *aleman* that they used to hold long conversations. The *aleman* had often said that he should aspire to go to Manila to study, and that he would make good because he would then cultivate further the inclination and the aptitude, that he acquired through exposure to better things. Time had a way of making resolutions fade, but the inclination remained, Camus would say, with a complacent shrug.

A few years back, a frequent visitor, the councilor for their area, offered him a *caminero's* job on a section of the municipal road to Cuenco. Camus still remembered the four short weeks of that only employment with an emotion akin to righteousness. He received thirty pesos for sweeping the road clean of stones and rubbish of which there was hardly any for the people scrupulously kept their dirt hidden in their backyards. It was the grass and the weeds that continually threatened to overrun the road. Then someone told him that the same councilor had placed someone else as a checker who had nothing to do but check on the camineros. With polite apologies to Meding and the baffled councilor, he left the job.

In the yard of their neighbor's house a group of young men began to gather. Laughter broke out often and once in a while someone slapped a neighbor on the back. Camus could make out nothing; the whirr of the crickets seemed to drown out all their talk. He sat at the window picking his teeth with his nails, a veined and hairy leg drawn up on the bench to support his chin. In the dusk, the group looked conspiratorial.

He looked long at Meding clearing the table. "You are right, I think," he said, half-asking.

Meding shrugged her frail shoulders. She crossed the wobbly bamboo bridge that connected their house to the old hut. Camus followed her without a word, wondering what she would do.

She led the way to the smaller of the two rooms. "I have prepared your white suit," she said.

She knelt before the wooden trunk, took a black key from the ring which always hung at her waist and twisted it into the keyhole. The suit lay on top of all the old clothes, like a silent, folded ghost in the lamplight, reminding Camus with a slight shock that it had been years since he wore it. The fragrance of its being kept in the trunk was wafted to him, redolent of an opulence he had never really enjoyed again after that morning of his wedding. Camus received it with some shyness. It was almost like a ritual and Camus was glad that the soft light hid his emotions.

All their life, sentiment had had very little meaning, perhaps because love had never figured in their courtship. Camus married Meding because his father and her father had agreed on the union. She had submitted impassively, although he had heard that she was a spirited girl. The vaunted spirit was to be known by him only through the regimen which she had imposed on their lives.

Sometimes when the barrenness of living engulfed him with a misery he could not understand, he felt that this was as it should be; life is hard, why should he complain, she was an ardent example of what hard work and frugality could bring. In his reveries he began to believe in the gladsome fullness of his life as the German had said it could be.

Camus held the coat before him. "It may no longer fit me," he said.

He felt that he had grown bigger, taller, more expansive in girth, so that when the coat slid easily over his shoulders and the pants hung loosely around his waist, consternation filled him. He realized that he had not really looked at himself for some time. He turned and lifted the lantern from the hook and walked slowly into the bigger bedroom where the three-paneled aparador stood.

The man in the mirror was someone whom he scarcely knew. He was stoop-shouldered, his chest caved in, and his silvery hair that stood erect in a close-cropped aguinaldo cut was sparse and revealed shiny brown scalp.

The face—taut and mask-like—shook him. He began to think that he would never, never be able to greet his hosts in the capitol with that boisterous warmth they themselves greeted him with when they mounted his stairs. Even if he had never intended to do so, he had long since learned that humility pleased his visitors.

So the suit did not really matter. All these years he thought he had really grown stout. He was still strong at the nets. He could lift sacks of rice with ease. Heavy loads never shortened his breath.

When his wife's face appeared from the shadows in the mirror, he felt even more saddened. He wondered, did she ever feel the need to look and live well, to experience heady well-being. Her lips drew back unsmiling, and as in answer to his thought, she spoke, her eyes betraying nothing: "You have not changed much. The years do not tell on you."

Camus stared at his image like it was a stricken adversary. He slowly unbuttoned the coat, dropped the pants and handed them back to Meding.

"Perhaps you had better put these back in the trunk." He looked at his wife in the mirror and in a voice that was not his, he told her that he could not go.

She listened to him indifferently; already in her mind, she was counting the chickens which she must catch, tie up and cage in stripped baskets. She knew how in the town every leaf of vegetable had its price and these would be her husband's levy. She had watched him welcome those people with touching sincerity that somehow made the patronizing tones of his guests sound boorish. And she, too, had acquiesced, having learned from dealing with merchants that sometimes yielding was the only way of getting your due.

"The young men are starting early in the morning. We must be up before the first cock crows," she said flatly, refusing to yield to the pleading in his eyes.

The crowd of women converged on Camus the moment he alighted from the bus, screaming and tugging at his two chicken coops. Then as suddenly as a swarm of flies that have found another victim, they dispersed leaving him with the empty containers and several smelly bills in his hands.

Camus stared at the money, then quickly pocketed it. He walked towards the church, not minding the crowd, the hawking vendors who thrust bundles of cake at his face.

Camus rubbed the back of his hand against his temples. Every step was taking him nearer to the superintendente's house and how could he go to him without the chicken? His throat was parched, the vendors thrust their wares at him again. *Pini-pig! Balut! Kropeck! Mais laga!* Above the voices, a tinkling bell now attracted him. He turned around; an ice cream vendor smiled at him: "Ice cream, sir! Ice cream!" They exchanged a look of understanding.

He watched the vendor pat layers of multi-colored ice cream into the cone. Yellow, violet, white. A final, careful pat of chocolate. He waved away the insistent hands and wares of the other peddlers. Slowly he drew the money from his pocket, picked the bill most frayed and gave it to the vendor. As he licked the ice cream, savoring the taste, he stretched out his hand for the change. All was quiet in the plaza now, and suddenly he realized that he had almost twenty pesos to spend as he pleased. He squinted craftily about him, seeing for the first time the enticements of the shops, hearing for the first time the loudspeakers talking to him alone. Yes, he must tell his wife how pleased the good lady had been, how truly fine a gentleman and friend the superintendente was.

Ines Taccad-Cammayo, mother of seven, earned her M.A. in English literature at Ateneo de Manila University. She has worked as a copywriter and editor, and now writes poetry, essays and short fiction. This story won first prize in the short story category of the Palanca Awards for Literature.

"But your grandmother pushed away those whispering
tempters, refused to be gainsaid and insisted
that you choose the harder course..."

The Dreams
of God's Children

BY JULIAN KAWALEC

THE first joy, a barely shadowy memory, was when you were lifted
onto the wagon and allowed to hold the reins; the second when
your father took you to a market stall and bought you a
pocketknife with a red pommeled handle; the third was probably
when, astride or rather alongside a horse, clinging to its dark mane
you forded a river; the fourth when you succeeded in grinding a
half-bushel of rye on a quern; the fifth when you discovered the
farm animals beginning to treat you seriously and obeying your
commands like a child his father's; the sixth when you suddenly
spotted your mother among the press of people and wagons in the
little town where you attended high school; the seventh when after
leaving high school you took a girl out in a boat for a row in a
small pond fenced off from the outside world by thick rushes and
went with her afterwards into those bushes and she let you have
your way; the eighth when out of the first meager pay packet
earned in that large university town you sent home five zlotys for

your mother to buy a paisley shawl and your father a supply of tobacco; the ninth when you turned down charity; the tenth was that spring day when, fleeing Gestapo bullets, you dived for cover into a field of ripening corn and got away; the eleventh when your mother found you in your hiding place and exclaimed, "You're alive and they said you were dead," and burst into tears; the twelfth when three hundred thousand Nazis were killed or captured at Stalingrad; the thirteenth when the war ended; the fourteenth when the landowners' estates were distributed among those who worked on them and stableboys hitched their own horses to their own wagons like real farmers; the fifteenth when your words appeared in print, in small black characters on gray sheets of newspaper; the sixteenth when you and a plump, copper-haired girl drove to your wedding; the seventeenth when that copper-haired girl said to you, "Put your hand on my belly," and you felt some living thing flutter beneath your touch; the eighteenth when your child was born; the nineteenth when your first book was published; the twentieth when you built a house.

Twenty memorable moments of joys...Obviously there have been more but these are the high points, the milestones between which are dotted a string of other, more minor pleasures. How many more will there be? A couple or so at most, so that all told you'll notch up twenty-odd, maybe twenty-five, principal joys—and that is your lifetime...

If I now wanted to list your sorrows and terrors, the first would surely be standing on an embankment as a child and watching a vast, raging tide of brown water with bits and pieces of buildings and dead animals and, perched on one plank, a white cat; at one point the plank was carried close enough to the dike for you to see that cat clearly, to watch it gather itself to leap to the safety of the embankment as the plank was swept nearer to its edge, but hesitating for fear of missing its footing or perhaps from hope of being carried even closer to dry ground; but it was not, for the water eddied, slowly but remorselessly, and bore it off towards its main current; and you remember that the further the cat receded the whiter it seemed to become until, sucked into the main current, it shone as brightly as a lamp and the further off it was borne by the flood the more brilliantly white it shone, an ever brighter twinkle on the dirty brown water which swept it on and on until with a final flicker it went out.

Then the whole world suddenly turned dark though it was broad daylight, but day had turned to night and the water had turned black as if transformed into pitch...

You clasped your grandfather's hand and leaned against him, standing there as though you had dozed off for a moment, but at once coming to and asking, "Why is it so dark?" and he replying, "But it's light," and you again asking, "Why is the water so black?" and he replying, "Black? It's simply in flood and dirty, because it's swollen after the rains and burst its banks."

"Did you see that cat?"

"There won't be any bread..."

"What could have become of that cat?"

"There may be a harvest on higher ground, but we're in for hard times."

"Cats are nimble. He could have jumped from the plank onto a wheatsheaf and from there to that rick of hay that was floating by..."

"If the people on the higher ground don't help us we're going to starve..."

"I bet he jumped onto that rick round the bend and is sitting there safe and sound."

"There's nothing left of last year's grain, not a husk even. How'll we feed the stock?"

"Cats don't need much of a foothold—he'll have leapfrogged out of trouble quick as a flash, won't he Grandpa?"

"The barn's empty except for the odd wisp of straw...merciful God..."

"Cats have nine lives..."

"God, my God..."

But there were more of these sorrows than joys and the skein to which you used to compare different events in life has more dark strands than gold. For shortly after the flood the cow died and you must have grieved, because when something like that happens the whole household grieves and the children have to take part in the grieving; even if they don't want to, their father will beat them into it, because when a cow dies there has to be grief; and then the black mare died, and later there was another flood, and a few years later prolonged rains, so heavy you couldn't find the sheafs which rotted in the fields and sprouted...

These sorrows followed in succession, one after another: disease struck the pigsties, the hogs and sows came out in pink spots and died like flies and, dead, looked as if their white skins had blossomed pink or someone, taking pity and paying them posthumous honors, had sprinkled them with rose petals...

Later a heifer impaled herself on a fence rail and then death visited your flesh and blood; Grandpa died; Grandma died, and how many sorrows were there in the schools you attended, though surely schools are a place where there shouldn't be any sorrows but there were, chiefly because schools were crying out for money and what they had wasn't enough...

The war doesn't even bear mentioning it's so obvious—death and death again, a hundred times, a million times over. The villages across the river were burned down, their inhabitants shot, your uncle was murdered in a camp—that strong, handsome uncle, tall and straight as a tree, the pride of the family, so strapping and clever and done to death in the prime of life by strangers from German towns or villages, Berlin, Munich or Frankfurt, perhaps from Mainz, or maybe from one of those picturesque villages where there are vineyards and the women sing as they gather the grapes, or perhaps from Lubeck, or perhaps from Bremen, God only knows where from, murdered by these people just like that, casually, and thrown into a furnace like firewood and burned to ashes...

When news came of his death the whole family, old and young, weeping quietly, drew together in a tight little knot because each sought from the other a solace that could not be given; and then they dispersed among the trees of the orchard and wept under their branches, and then suddenly they all reassembled, trooped into the barn, closed the doors and thus shielded from the stares of onlookers, burst into loud wails and a barn which had recently rung with the music of flails turned into a weeping barn.

Father arrived later because he had been helping a neighbor with the delivery of a calf since there had been complications with its birth and who knows how it might have turned out if it had not been for Father who knew almost everything about animal disorders, and calving in particular.

When he opened the doors, the first thing he did, dazed from the exertions and tensions he had just been through assisting at that birth, was to cry out, breathing heavily, "I had my workout, the calf was crooked," as if he hadn't heard the weeping and groaning; it was only after a while that he joined in the grief, but without weeping, mourning only silently, and then, stretching out his arms, his sleeves still rolled up from his business in the neighbor's cowshed and streaked with unwashed blood, said: "Do not weep—it must have been God's will;" everyone quietened down a little, some wiped away their tears and stopped lamenting...

Uncle's youngest niece was one of those who wiped away their tears, but she did so with an air of anger, as though she were rebelling deep down and answered Father with a question: "Where is God? Why does He do nothing?" and then seemingly less angrily, "You're not here, God."

On hearing this, Grandfather quickly wiped away his tears and shouted:

"Don't blaspheme, girl! God exists..."

"If He does," she replied, "He's on the side of Nazis if He let them murder Uncle..."

"It was His will."

"How could it be?"

"None of your lip, brat!" shouted my aunt who on hearing her daughter had quickly wiped away her tears.

"God moves in mysterious ways..." said Grandfather thoughtfully.

"What kind of ways are ones that make good, wise people die in torment!"

"Cut it out, you brat! Kneel down and pray, and beg God's forgiveness!" Grandfather again shouted and raised his bony, mottled hand in which he held a twisted length of binding twine,

"Kneel or I'll whip you!"

"I will not!"

Grandmother, sobbing, stepped over to her, put her hand on her head, stroking her blond, flat-brushed hair, slid her hand down the plait that hung to her waist and said softly, beseechingly: "Kneel, kneel—you've sinned grievously," and then Uncle's younger niece knelt down on the hard floor and started to pray and make strenuous supplication to God:

"O God, may the men who murdered my uncle never return to their homes and never see their own hearths, and may they die in torment and be a long time dying and suffer terrible pain and may no one agree to put them out of their misery, and when they are dead may they go to the bottomest pit of hell where the devils will flay the skin off their bodies..."

She stopped and at once an argument broke out because Grandmother said that this was no kind of prayer to address to God while Father believed it was; "After what's happened it is," he said; he was backed up by Mother who declared, "At a time when such terrible things are going on in the world I think you can make such a prayer." But Grandmother was unconvinced and objected, "God cannot hobnob with the Devil and urge him to flay Gestapomen..."

All of a sudden the news that Uncle was dead again toppled on them in all its enormity and once more they broke down beneath its weight and wept...

You rushed forward and lamented and lamented, but what else could you do when, breaking all the rules in this narrative, you have jumpcut to the war and cannot extricate yourself from it. Reluctant as you are to recollect those wartime years, you cannot help yourself and your memory drags you back to them in spite of yourself; and so once again it is nineteen-hundred and forty-five because that is a year which keeps recurring in your thoughts. It is winter and you have found your way to the scene of the fighting for the liberation of the Coast, you are in Gdansk—and don't brag that you're there with a rifle, because all you have is a reporter's pen, even if you carry it like a rifle—T-34s trundle down a street heaped with rubble, teetering over the mounds of debris, rearing up on their hind legs, gun barrels pointing to the sky, then plunging and dipping their barrels to the hot earth, occasionally one stops, an invisible gunner swings the barrel to a target, fires, the steel hulk trembles, the barrel puffs smoke and slowly, gingerly, inches forward again; mopping up the last Nazi pockets of resistance—that's what I think you called it in your copy for the *Polpress Bulletin*...

The tanks recede into the distance and their clatter fades away among the ruins and smoke, shooting becomes increasingly sporadic and suddenly there is silence in this empty, lifeless, shattered street, but a brief silence because a strong wind blew up from the sea and poured into the street, singing in various keys; it fluted musically through holes and cracks in the walls, clanged on buckled metal and moaned over ripped cables; and at the same time it swept the street, clearing it of dust, bringing the rubble and the corpses of people and horses into stark relief, unshrouding the lifelessness; it tore into houses abandoned in panic by their fleeing owners, laid open by shells, indecently exposed, their most private secrets revealed, and burst into kitchens, bedrooms and parlors and began spewing out all sorts of objects: out fluttered clothes, sheets and tablecloths, out tumbled toys and pots and pans, hats danced on the air borne up by the whirls and gusts of the wind as though looking for their heads, ballooning nightdresses, their sleeves outspread, seemed to be pursuing the naked bodies of mislaid women...

Occasionally, a piece of furniture—a cupboard, a bed, a sideboard—standing on the edge of a floor tipped over and fell with a crash on the rubble in the roadway...

A large looking glass, miraculously all in one piece, not even scratched, as clean as polished silver, began to inch down a slanting plank and, lying on its back, was halted for a moment by a tangle of wiring protruding from a wall which, quivering like a spring, gently, as though aware it was a fragile object, nudged it on to a strip of metal roof covering down which it carefully, avoiding all harm, slid to ground level and, coming to rest at the bottom, tilted itself upright normally as you please, as though holding itself in readiness for the whole city, for anyone and anything that might wish to see how they looked...

This opportunity was promptly taken by a horse lying just opposite on the shattered concrete, still hitched to the shaft of a smashed wagon, one of those smallish but tough and incredibly durable Caucasian breeds with thick manes that fall over their foreheads and ripple as they gallop. Maybe he had seen several years of army service, in various branches, but probably had been used most often to pull ammunition wagons, missing meals, missing sleep, because he had to deliver his shells in time, always in harness, always on the move, always pressing on with that long loping stride which is the best for covering long distances, a hundred kilometers or more a day, for artillery must fire and machine guns spray bullets; from the Caucasus he had set out and come all the way to Gdansk and so many times, maybe a thousand, the flying bullets had missed him, whistled past his ear and missed, but in Gdansk one had found its mark and now he lay there peacefully, resting on the stones and examining himself in an elegant looking-glass, peering through the slits of unclosed lids, baring his teeth as though in a grin, the wind ruffling his mane and tossing it in thick strands over his forehead; he must like what he sees because he keeps gazing into that mirror, staring at it as though asking: What will you tell me, what will you tell me?

And at once there gathered to examine themselves in that clean, undamaged looking-glass other dead horses, and dead men and women, and ruins and heaps of rubble, soldiers blinded by fire and eyeless houses stared at their reflection, and wounds and things that hurt examined themselves in that single looking-glass standing among the devastation, the whole war saw there its ashen, haunted features, its bloodstained, suppurating face...

That mirror stood and stood there and everything before it gazed into its glass and it was the only clean thing on that dun-colored, dingy day of the war...

Now it's a haggard, emaciated man who approaches the looking-glass, not quite a soldier, not quite a civilian, not quite young, not quite old, but looking more young than old, clothed in tatters which might once have been a uniform, and shod not in boots but rags with those brown splotches usually left by old bloodstains, bareheaded, fair hair caked, plastered to his skull, a narrow, dirty face, forehead also streaked with those brown stains, eyes sunk deep into the head, crowned by white brows...

He must have crawled out of the cellar of some ruin in which he had long been trapped and on unsteady feet, stumbling over the debris, slowly shuffled toward the mirror which as soon as he had clambered out of his lair, had captured and submerged his reflection in its spotless transparency; and now, as he approached the looking-glass, he simultaneously emerged from it, that is walked towards himself, there is one of him but also two, each identical, and he can see himself exactly and even converse with himself, and be told what he is really like for mirrors don't lie, not ones of such peerless quality....

He is puzzled by his own appearance as he approaches that sheet of glass, exceedingly bewildered: "*Herr Gott, das ist unmöglich,* it's impossible, impossible that I could have changed that much. How on earth, *Herr Gott,* could the *Herr Übermensch* be so altered, clad in tatters stained with coagulated blood and starving? What's become of the uniform, the cap with the death's head, the belt inscribed *Gott mit uns,* where's the riding crop, the gleaming black-barreled Walther which has killed a hundred mothers, a hundred sons and fathers, dispatched a hundred husbands and children, and young girls who had barely blossomed, where's that revolver which defied the whole world?

"*Brot, etwas Brot, ein Krümchen Brot,*" he said to you beseechingly as he turned away from the looking-glass, empty hand outstretched like a beggar; and then tried to say it in Polish or possibly Russian and stammered out: "Kleb, kleb."

"Should I, Grandma, advise me, because I don't know whether to give him a piece of bread or not?" In my mind's eye I saw my grandmother because it was bread that was involved, it's always been like that—ever since, I suppose, I fetched up on the other side of the river, on the threshold, that is, of a new stone world and a new life—that whenever I hear the word bread it rings in my ears like an echo of that erstwhile, old-time "bread" spoken so often, so many countless times by my grandmother, like an echo winging across time as if it were a huge forest or mountain chain...

There cannot have been a word spoken as many times in her long life as the word bread, no other word can compete with it, it stood at the very summit of the grandmother tongue and cracked the whip over the rest of her vocabulary, governed the whole of the grandmother tongue: "Look after the bread, don't scatter the bread, pick up that slice of bread and kiss it, apologize for dropping it, go on, say you're sorry or I'll tan your hide; bread, more bread, you greedy kids? The rain's falling and the bread unharvested; the river's swollen like a sea and the bread uncollected; tuck that bread away in case someone steals it from you; he drowned trying to rescue the bread; here you are again begging for bread, I'm sure you want it for the foal and that's a sin; they killed him for the bread he was carrying; the whole loaf was splashed with blood, but they wiped it off and ate it, they that were breadless..."

No other word can overtake bread in her speech, perhaps only *God* can keep up; God is probably just a pace behind and sometimes even neck and neck, but even then bread has its nose out front, and God is only backup, used for thanksgiving or supplication in sudden necessity and also for the most cautious and tactful of reproaches: "The bread's safe in the barn, thank God, so much bread carried away by flood, how could You, God? Thy will be done, the sheaves are a swamp, the bread is a swamp, God have mercy on us, come on, have mercy! Avert that cloud, dear God, or the bread will go to waste, this cold spell is bad for the bread, dear God, drought—what will become of the bread, my God?"

If she were canonized—and canonized she deserves to be—who, I'd like to know, so gallantly stood watch over the bread? All sorts of princesses and queens have been canonized though they did little enough, but she still awaits canonization—if she were made a saint she should be called Saint Eve of the Bread—and holy pictures should represent her emerging from a larder, tiny and wizened, her face burned by sun and sleet, with a loaf clutched to her breast, cradling the bread as though it were alive, not a thing, but a creature; toting that bread which is big and she tiny, insignificant compared to that bread, overshadowed by that bread, tiny, but strong enough to carry that great bread, that's how she should be depicted when she is canonized...

I thought of her so intently that I saw her climbing out of her grave and stepping over to me, standing beside me on the ruins of the city of Gdansk; and it seemed to me that together with her I looked down at that übermensch laid low and beseeching bread...

"I hate to admit it," she said, "but I feel sorry for him; we'll give him bread, but first we'll gather our people so that they can watch you giving him bread and him eating it..."

At once a whole throng poured out of houses and graves like an audience gathering to see a show, but there was nothing remarkable about the spectacle; I simply handed him the bread which he seized greedily and began to eat, wolfing it like a hungry man, but also ordinarily like anyone who is hungry, cramming huge bites into his mouth till his cheeks puffed out and then swallowing and continually bowing and saying, *Danke*. Nothing much was happening, but the crowd looked on with bated breath before dispersing back to houses and graves...

Dispersed too are your nearest and dearest, but they have always been standing by for a summons, ever vigilant in their houses and graves, ever peering with the transfixing gaze of the longsighted through mysterious cracks, and seeing you from their hiding places among willow thickets and tall stands of wheat, and churchyard birches which eternally weep and lament, you cannot escape them, they'll catch up with you, plonk themselves down in your city home, squat at the foot of your bed because they want to know what you are doing and what dreams you have...

However, some of this imagined throng of kith and kin from across the river and from the valley watching you give bread to the übermensch went off disgruntled because they would have preferred you to make an end of that hungry übermensch instead of feeding him; and they, particularly that youngest cousin of yours, the son of the uncle shot in the forest, that cousin who secretly plotting revenge was ripped apart by a grenade, whispered in your ear before you followed your grandmother's advice and held out that bread to the übermensch: "Don't give him bread and don't play at being noble, but make an end of him, take that captured Walther revolver, aim the barrel which for so long was pointed at us in the opposite direction and kill him, go on, kill him, that will be justice…"

But your grandmother pushed away those whispering tempters, refused to be gainsaid and insisted that you choose the harder course, that is, give bread to a hungry man; and then she stepped back a little way till she stood on a pile of debris like some outlandish preacher and for the umpteenth time told you not to kill that übermensch…

"Squirt bread into him, not a bullet, Grandson," she cried in a resounding voice, standing on that bizarre pulpit, till the echo rang through the streets of the city of Gdansk filled with the stench of death, piled with chunks of masonry and the ironmongery of destroyed tanks and guns, strewn with the corpses of men and horses, streets which could only be called that on account of the still upstanding walls of gutted houses, through which swept a chill, maritime wind, screaming like the damned and carrying the echo of Grandmother's sermon the length and breadth of Gdansk, the length and breadth of the sea, the length and breadth of the world…

And in this sermon Grandmother set her sights on something that has defeated both saints in heaven and saints on earth, something that has been and continues to be too much even for God himself: to try and persuade people to trade blows not of steel and fire, but of bread, to put an end for good to wars in which blood is shed, men kill each other out of hatred and corpses pile up, and embark instead on *wars* of a benign, agreeable and attractive kind in which people will pelt each other with bread…

Grandmother, whom you imagined in the ruins of Gdansk, dug in her heels and resolved to secure an objective that has been beyond the capacities of both heavenly forces and the wisest and most noblest of souls on earth…

"What good, my beloved grandson," she addressed me in the course of her sermon, "what good will it do to avenge the death of your uncle, loving nephew that you are, and kill that übermensch? If you do that, you may later find a nephew or son of that German lying in wait to kill you, to avenge the death of his uncle or father, and then your nephew or son will lie in wait for the nephew or son of that German; and then the nephew or son of the nephew or son of that German will lie in wait for the nephew or son of your nephew or son and the result will be that there will never be an end to killing and revenge will succeed revenge to the end of time..."

That grandmother, an ordinary old peasant woman, as weak and fragile as a willow twig, but also as tireless and stubborn as a willow twig, dared to try and stop the torrent of blood which the naïve or disingenuous have given the dignified name of history...

But how could Grandmother succeed in an attempt that had defeated the joint efforts of sages, saints and God? She was attempting the impossible and accomplished no more than that her grandson listened to her, after which everything went its own way...

For when the guns grew silent, God's children—God's because they have reportedly been made in God's image and likeness—applied themselves with vast industry to the development of increasingly efficient means of killing each other and demolishing homes; and God's children are overjoyed at possessing such marvelous devices which can kill any man fifteen times over, that is, kill fifteen times more people than inhabit the globe and can destroy fifteen planets like the earth...

But that is not enough for these children of God made, as the Bible states in black and white, in His image and likeness, and so they are doing their utmost, working round the clock, to acquire the capability to kill every inhabitant of the earth sixteen times over; and now God's children, devout, prayerful children who worship deities and ideals, who love birds, poetry and music, have their hearts set on mini-instruments of mega-destruction and would be only too happy if something no bigger than, say, an apple, pear or Havana cigar, could on explosion devastate an average-sized city and kill all its inhabitants; what joy would there be among God's children if they invented something like that and how much more delighted would God's children be if they could devise a ray as fine as a hair or even finer and this ray projected from a great distance could pierce and topple mountains and blow houses into little pieces, quite apart from killing people; such a ray would represent a clean death, without bloodshed and the unpalatable sight of shattered bodies; no changes, no ugly blotches, no crushings, only a slight paling of faces and immobility; infliction of such a clean, snow-white death, such simple, hygienic liquidation of God's children, is the dream of God's children...

Born in 1916, Julian Kawalec graduated from the Department of Polish Philology at the Jagiellonian University. He worked as a journalist. His literary debut was in 1957 with several short stories. Since then there has been a flow of short stories and novels, some of which have been translated into as many as 16 languages. He has been awarded numerous literary prizes, and is a member of the Society of European Culture and the PEN Club. His skilled translator is Edward Rothert.

"Those animals will bring lots of people, I suppose,
but there are lots of things that have
to be taken into account."

El Circo

BY PEDRO JUAN SOTO

*RADIO WATCH: Today in the town of Centeno, four men were
shot to death and many others wounded when they attacked
the Romero Circus. The police state that the motive for the
attack remains a mystery, although they have ruled out robbery.
Stay tuned to RADIO WATCH for further updates on this
tragedy.*

"How did you do it?" the investigator asked.
"Out in the hills."
"I didn't say where, I said how."
The four-sided corral, improvised under the glaring lights of the
enormous tent for the two ruminants, contained three basins of
water and a large cardboard box filled with hay. They were
ruminants from the mountains, defenseless animals, now enclosed
in the small town.
The investigator went back to his notes.

"You're Alex, right? Alex González."

"Yessir. Trapeze artist."

"And you," said the investigator, turning toward the massive black man, "you helped in the hunt."

"I'm the strong man and I do lots of things in the Romero Circus. Yes, I helped to collar those damned animals. Luispé and Desi pitched in too."

"Luispé?"

"Luispé went to get the boss. You sure ask a lotta questions an' we ain't done nothin'...Desi's probably in the kitchen makin' coffee."

The investigator looked at his watch and walked around the pen once more. The animals had little buds of horns, rather hunched backs, seedy-looking coats that went right up to their jaws, small feet, and long tails.

"How do they protect themselves?" he asked.

Alex showed his bandaged left hand, which he'd kept out of sight.

"With their teeth and their hooves, mister."

"And their tails, do they use them like whips?"

"Well they stick 'em up in the air," said the black man coming forward, "but if they ever tried to use 'em on me, I swear they'd be deep-fried right now."

The investigator applauded quietly as he noted the reaction of the ruminants. Both remained with their eyes closed in the middle of the corral, stock still, simply ruminating.

"Besides hay, did you give them any corn to eat?"

"Mister, they ain't chickens," said the short trapeze artist. Then he burst out laughing.

The investigator didn't laugh. When he clapped his hands, the animals didn't react. Could they be deaf? How badly were they hurt before they were caught?

Two men suddenly came into the tent before the investigator could ask any more questions. The fatter of the two, coat on, stretched out his right hand:

"Charlie Romero, at your service. This is Angel Luis Pérez, Luispé. Can I help you?"

"How do. I'm an investigator for the SPCA. Some of your neighbors here have complained."

"Complaints? I'm shocked." Charlie pulled up his coat, which was slipping off his shoulders, and straightened his tie. "These dangerous animals have been very well tended since last Sunday, when my men caught them. We've given them a home, and people have come—even brought their children—to see them. There's no danger to anyone, not a bit. We're breaking them in, training them, so they'll be the pride of the Romero Circus and of Puerto Rico. The hunt was a success, a real adventure. The newspapers were here already, don't you read the papers?"

"How many more days do you plan to be here?" the investigator asked.

"We've been here a week already, but with these stupendous animals I think we'll probably stay on for at least 20 more days. At first we didn't make out very well, but now we've caught on. Somebody jealous must have spread the story that these poor animals are causing problems, but it's just not true. We always leave someone here all night to watch out for them."

The investigator walked slowly toward the exit, followed by Charlie. "I have to go back to Ponce," he said. "Next week I'll turn in my report. I don't know what decisions will be taken, but I am concerned about the sanitary conditions of those two creatures, Mister Romero."

"Sanitary conditions? We worry like hell about just that, my friend. We are decent folks, you know. You go back to your 'Society' or whatever you call it and tell them. We believe in protecting everyone. You won't let me down now, will you?"

When they reached the investigator's car, Charlie tried to shake hands with him, but the investigator suddenly pulled his hand back. At their feet fell a rolled up $50 bill.

"You're mistaken," said the investigator, smiling as he settled into the driver's seat and Charlie picked up the cash. "Believe me when I tell you I don't want to hurt you or your circus. Those animals will bring in lots of people, I suppose, but there are lots of things that have to be taken into account. Good-bye, Mister Romero."

The car slowly pulled away from the circus grounds and the gigantic tent. He hadn't spoken with the mayor yet, but apparently the circus people had followed orders and had not disturbed town life by setting up their circus right in the town square.

A few hundred meters from the area where the circus was, the streets of the town began. Several of the locals were waiting on the sidewalk, but no one stopped the investigator to ask anything when he drove by.

AP: Two employees of the Romero Circus were killed by machete-wielding assailants today when a riot broke out in Centeno, a town located in the interior of Puerto Rico. Desiderio Cartagena, a native of Cayey, and Angel Luis Pérez, from Santurce, vainly tried to fight off more than 1200 angry individuals who apparently wanted to remove them from the lot the circus had been allowed to use during the festivities honoring Centeno's patron saint. Two more victims are Pablo Casiano, of Ponce, and Lucas Ordóñez, from Villalba.

According to the police report, the riot was provoked by the stench produced by two rare animals, called singalús, *which the Romero Circus was training in Centeno at the time.*

Four streets laid out crosswise, that's Centeno. Everybody goes to church because the church has been like the supermarket since they built the first two or three houses, you get the picture? We came from the north and we had a hard time, but we kept going even though things got even worse after the hunt.

González, Alex. Trapeze artist, Romero Circus. I was born in Santurce, Puerto Rico, in 1957. I've been working here for nine months, with no fringe benefits, but I never had better friends than Desi the Magician, Julio the Strong Man, and the owner Charlie. The other people are important too, but there's a lot of them and I don't want to go down the list one by one because you already know them, and my statement would just end up a list of names, right? If you want to know something about someone in particular, ask me later.

This town is shit, okay? Never a word of thanks, and we busted balls to give 'em a treat. I never forget the bad things people do, but I never say anything because I'm not the kind of guy who likes to get into fights.

The idea was Charlie's. Charlie told us to catch six *sagalús* or *sagaluses*. The circus was gonna go bust if it didn't have a big draw, you get me?

So we're out in the hills. It's six in the morning and we got into town yesterday at four in the afternoon, okay? We had some salami and cheese sandwiches and water which we finished off after we were there for five hours.

The little old man Charlie hired as a guide was more lost than we were. He'd take a squint and then say he didn't remember. He'd talk a lot to cover up and so Charlie would pay him later and not chew him down. He was smart but we had his number. "There used to be a ravine over there," he said, "but it was washed out in the last storm. I had more hair the last time I came up these hills"—he'd say—"but my tongue was just as long." That's the kinda thing he'd say while we'd be standing there with our mouths shut. Of all of us I was the one who talked with the old guy the most while we were on the watch, and I could see that he didn't know a thing about *sagalús,* okay? Then Julio started up and told dirty jokes, and we all took a little nap, mosquitoes and all. Mister, I'm telling you we took it on the neck out there that morning. The old geezer was talking about the swamps over where the cattails were, and we listened, but that was when the sun came up. Julio and I said no thanks and looked at each other again. We talked for a bit, stretched out next to each other. Let's go back man, that's the best thing, f–k these animals. But what's going on back there? Julio was crazy thinking about getting another woman, one he'd already seen in town. He said if he got back early he'd catch her nice and warm in bed because her husband worked in Arecibo. Not me. I got divorced six years and four months ago. That didn't turn me off all the way, but I wasn't much in the mood to take out another license, got me? And I didn't see anything great in that burg.

At about ten in the morning the thing began for real. We saw one—his big ears and his long tail—but he disappeared without coming close. According to Charlie and the old geezer, this kind of game always goes around in packs of 15 or 20. Julio and I were really scared out there in the hills. The old man kept saying that patience is a virtue. Julio looked at me and I looked at that sky.

Then four turned up at around noon and the third stale sandwich of the day. The way I was I would have eaten 'em all without even cooking 'em. Julio said something about roping 'em, but I wouldn't do it even if I was a cowboy. I stayed put: I make my living on the trapeze.

UPI: For the past 24 hours, a prosecutor for the Special Investigations Department (SID) has been questioning three members of the Romero Circus about the riot that took place in Centeno, a town situated in the southern foothills of the Central Mountains. The prosecutor, Josué Ferré, has taken statements from Carlos Romero Barceló, 50 years old; Julio César Andrades, 30; and Alejandro González Malavé, 21 years old. The owner of the circus, Romero, is accused of provoking the tragic conflict in Centeno which resulted in two dead and many wounded.

In the center of Centeno, which is the county seat, you can see the church and the plaza. The town was founded in 1801. The church was built in 1802 and almost right afterward the plaza, where the women walk on the left side because the men took over the right side a long time back. From the center of town sprouted two streets like two branches and from those two branches two more sprouted later.

No part of the branch streets had been set aside for business. The founders of the town—genuinely devout folks—built their houses there so they could watch over the progress of the church that was being built. Their houses were like minarets proclaiming both divine glory and the good name of the settlement. The long streets became crowded with little shops—bakeries, fried-food stands, miserable dairy shops that little by little grew taller than the original houses. Ours is a scrawny town, more rocks than trees, more sand than blood. One thing we've got a lot of is envy.

The church of San Jacinto has distinguished itself almost from the day it was founded because the priests and their respective housekeepers have taken in numerous orphans. Their first names have been Jesus, Jacinto, Venancio, José (the names of the priests at San Jacinto, according to the town gossips).

Our town is small—there are some 13,500 people here, between the town itself and the four outside villages—and full of feuds. The foothills of the Central Mountains lie to the north. The village of Hato Calizo has always had around 1,000 inhabitants: farm workers who work here some and then a lot in New Jersey. Every six months they come back to stretch out in their hammocks, yawn, drink, and plant seeds that never take.

Verde Arriba, with Hato Calizo on one side and the hills on the other, has 1,500 inhabitants. These people are just as unproductive as the folks in Hato Calizo, except that they make wooden saints that they try to sell down in the town. They don't sell many. The women from Verde Arriba, however, are highly prized in the town because they have strong legs and rosy cheeks: They're called the peaches-and-cream girls. Verde Abajo is a bit more respectable from the point of view of the town because even though it only has 1,500 inhabitants it has a lot of men and produces lots of electricians. This village, bounded on the north by Hato Calizo and on the northeast by Verde Arriba, even though it, too, lacks running water, is feuding with Centeno and is really going at it with the village called Zorzal, which is on the other side of the town.

The dispute arises from the fact that the people in Centeno are either old people or their heirs, not one of whom does an honest day's work (according to the Verde Abajo folks), and in Zorzal there are only ironworkers who know little about plumbing and even less about building houses and highways. The population of Zorzal—6,000 inhabitants—is not only larger than that of Verde Abajo but is actually twice the size of that of Centeno itself, which only has a population of 3,000. Centeno is at odds with Zorzal not only because Zorzal wants to be the county seat, but because Zorzal has grown as a result of an influx of new people from other nearby towns.

97

Our town is small and full of feuds, more sand than blood, and our problems have grown. The mayor, poor devil, has allowed the Romero Circus to set up in the Zorzal neighborhood.

RADIO WATCH: The number of wounded after the violent incident that occurred in Centeno recently has risen to 58. Those requiring hospitalization are in Juana Diaz, Ponce and Coamo. One of the wounded refuted published reports about the riot against the Romero Circus, of which nothing remains but ruins today. Roberto Valentín Pereira, a native of Coamo and 35 years of age, declares that he and others present during the festivities in honor of the patron saint of Centeno marched toward the Romero Circus in order to complain about the cries of the two sagalús—animals that are half deer, half pony—that were tortured by employees of the Romero Circus. When they arrived at the circus and demanded pity for the two beasts, Valentín Pereira goes on to say, they were fired upon by the circus people and, in his own words, "We had to get back at them with whatever we could lay our hands on." The police say that the animals had been butchered and were found in large pots of boiling water when the townspeople managed to enter the Romero Circus's main tent.

We were coming from Caguas, where we'd only lasted four or seven days. We went to the coast, which took us to Arecibo: nice, understanding people. We stayed there maybe fourteen days. The next stop would have been Aguadilla or Mayagüez, but I decided that the best thing for my circus would be the interior. We went on to Utuado and Jayuya, and it was then I realized that the trip was turning into a perfect flop. In Utuado I had to let six guys go and in Jayuya eight more good men said good-bye. We spent 20 days in those parts, sometimes with a dozen people in the audience and never more than 30 kids who came to laugh at Calcalero the clown.

My circus was big, huge, until then. The big top could hold about 250 people. Adults paid a dollar, kids fifty cents. We had a lion that wowed them in Caguas, Arecibo, and Utuado. All of a sudden he died on us after a fit of diarrhea. I never doubted for a minute that somebody had poisoned him.

We were in Centeno where all that stuff happened for maybe fifteen days—not doing great but not starving either. We're all good people here, all eager to please. And we work hard, 'cause we're fanatics about doing our jobs and doing them right. We don't do a thing unless we have an artistic reason for doing it, unless it helps us to make our public happy so we can earn our daily bread.

I mean I had 22 people to feed every day and to pay each month. I also had the usual circus animals: two trained monkeys, a baby elephant, and a show horse. I was the one who supervised setting up whenever we got to a new town, after requesting a permit from the mayor and paying for it. Transportation was also my lookout. There were eight of us left when we landed in Centeno. The people greeted us like long lost brothers, probably because nobody'd been there in God knows how long. The festival of the patron saint had always been as much fun as stepping on a cowpat, to use the local expression.

We changed things for the good—the mayor told me himself. We never dreamed we'd be fighting for our lives, because we're peaceful folks. We don't do bad things. Just the opposite, we bring happiness and excitement. I've been in this game since I was 18 and I'm now just over 50, if you don't mind me saying so. We don't know what happened, but just as there are good people there are bad ones, too, and envious people and people who call us intruders. I asked, that's all I did, I asked for some animals from the hills, I didn't know then that the animals from the mountains were animals people loved. Someone said they were rare animals, never seen from close up by the citizens of this honorable community. We weren't doing badly, but not that well either, and I figured that I had to have something in my circus that would draw these people in.

And people began to turn out as soon as we brought in those animals, which are neither horses nor mules. They were an attraction, why not? Sometimes they would walk around calmly and other times they hunkered down on the ground. We asked the kids not to feed them and we asked the parents to watch out for the kids. That was how a new triumph began for us. That was also the end of the complaints, the bitterness and the nightmares of all the employees who were left.

UPI: One of the individuals involved in the Centeno riot declared that he and his comrades acted in self-defense after an attack by a drunken mob that kept them from getting ready for the Romero Circus's next show.

Calixto Calero, better known as Calcalero the Clown, states: "It was a mob, get me? I was putting on my makeup and didn't know what was happening. The show must go on; besides it was our work. Four or six guys appeared with rocks and sticks. What were we going to do, throw flowers at them? I hit the floor and took out my gun—I've got a license to carry a revolver."

Calcalero the Clown has more than 20 years' experience in the circus. "Everybody likes me, young and old," he added, "because I've performed in the United States and even on television."

How did I get to be the strong man? Sometimes I wonder. I was a boxer. But I quit after a few good fights. I could have gone on, but I didn't think I had much of a chance as a heavyweight. And I didn't really want to move down to middleweight. I figured I had to survive, you know what I mean? To keep on going down this long road, always hopin' for something better. Know what it is to take a shot right in the heart, on the side of your head, do ya? I took a couple in the head, but none in my heart. I just kept saying: hold on. That's what you've got to do, stand up and start punching. If you don't, you're yellow. That's why I had to shoot.

Just imagine that someone's breaking into your house, your own house. Well, the Romero Circus's been my house now for more than nine years. You just don't stand by and let 'em do what they want, 'cause in this country a man's gotta prove he's a man. And they killed two of us—Luispé and Desi—all because they didn't do what I told 'em to do. Two martyrs. I cried my eyes out at their funeral remembering the good times we all had together: Desi the

Magician, when he kept us all alive the time he did his tricks for some hick town when we were with the Lausel Circus. Luispé, the High Wire Walker, who always walked on a wire with electricity running through it. Those guys were my teachers from the Lausel Circus days. How could I know that some day I was gonna work with them, my teachers? Two martyrs. But I don't see you arresting any of the guys who attacked us, and the badge you show me says you represent justice.

Putting it all together, the whole thing began with the hunt and ended with the screams of those animals. The town got upset. The whole business was unnecessary, by the way. It was Alex's idea, I mean roasting them. We were washing the *sagalús* in the pots so we could roast them whole later, but then those people came in screaming just like the animals in the pots. What should I have done? We all have to eat, right? Those people didn't know nothing about nothing. Assholes—but don't record that, okay?

When we went out to the hills, we knew that the circus was on its last legs, that Centeno couldn't pay the Romero Circus's expenses, that we'd already been there a long time and that the patron saint deal wasn't gonna give us much. We were gonna move on to I don't know where. That's how it was, nothing at all like what Desi and Luispé told me the way things were with the Lausel Circus.

Some people got drunk, that's a fact. We called in the police. There were a lot of us, between the animals and the keepers. Desi was a magician, but he doubled as a cook; Angel Luis Pérez used to try to help him out. And Desi, looking at the *sagalús,* said, "The truth is that they stink. But you know what they say: he who doesn't buy food doesn't eat. What do you say we wash 'em down and roast 'em?" It all started as a joke, see? Some things you can figure out, of course, but even though we'd all had a few drinks, no one could see what was gonna happen when Luispé and Desi—may God have mercy on their souls—started petting those *sagalús.*

You're at home and then something happens. You hear shouting outside and inside. We tried to cut off the shouts from inside and we did. But the outside shouts got louder. You're at home. We had guns, but we'd never touched them before. Not even out in the hills, because we captured those two things with our bare hands. Okay, Alex is nervous. But when Charlie, Luispé, and Desi grabbed the shotguns, there was no reason to follow them. I got into a corner, not because I'm yellow, but I got into a corner anyway. The townspeople had their complaints: the stink, the screams, and before that, the way those *sagalús* cry all the time. You expect the worst when people force their way into your house, you grab what you can and fight to show them that you're still alive, right?

When I was boxing I would go into a corner. Tactics. That way I could catch my breath. I caught a lot of flak for that, but who cared? I stayed fine and was able to come out ready for the next contract.

Anyway, when we came down from the hills, Charlie pulled that "And what did you do, Julito?" stuff. I threw my towel in his face to shut him up. That's the way we left it, because if he said something more he wouldn't have been able to waltz around so easy. About the other jerks I also would not want to talk seriously.

AP: The Natural Resources Department is carrying out an investigation into the brutal murder of two ruminant mammals captured and butchered by members of the Romero Circus in the town of Centeno. The killing of the two animals on the night of July 25 drove the local citizens and others drawn to Centeno by curiousity to seek revenge. The Centeno riot ended in four dead and more than 50 wounded. The butchered animals were known as sagalús, *according to the Natural Resources Department, and they represented a species almost extinct on the island of Puerto Rico. The* sagalús, *despite their fringed tails, resemble deer. They have long, thin feet and fluted horns.*

He smoked as he sharpened pencils in his room at the Meliá Hotel. For two hours, returning from Centeno, he had been writing down notes about his findings, and that made him feel even more fatigued and frustrated.

It was nightfall in Ponce, a city that never gladdened his heart. The lights in the Degetau Plaza had been on since much earlier. He didn't really feel like eating supper. He smoked and sharpened unnecessary pencils. He would not go back to Centeno, someone else would have to take over the investigation. He had done half the job. He was worried that he hadn't demanded that the Centeno police take charge of the *sagalús*, but the SPCA contract said nothing about facing up to a bunch of thugs from a circus that had invaded some hick town. Somebody else would have to get a judge to hand down that court order.

Because it was a holiday he didn't call the board of directors. And they hadn't given him their home phone numbers either. He wouldn't work for them anymore.

He placed his portable typewriter on the shaky, chipped table, gathered together the pencils and put his notes in order. He put a sheet of paper into the typewriter and began to type:

To: The Board of Directors, SPCA.
From: José A. Salazar, Investigator.
Subject: Cruelty to Ruminants,
*   Centeno, P.R.*
Date: July 25, 1978.

The complaints forwarded to the SPCA have turned out to be justified, as my findings reveal. I have spent the day investigating the Romero Circus and the town of Centeno, which is in the judicial zone of Ponce.

Five days ago, the staff of the Romero Circus seized two ruminants in the hills surrounding Centeno. The ruminants, known in those parts as Sagalús, apparently do quite well on a diet of grass and water. They are rare animals and resemble ponies with twisted tails which they use as whips. They possess light coats, rather like fine horsehair, strong hooves and pointy snouts.

These two seem to have been mistreated since they were brought to the site of the Romero Circus. They have lost hooves, their long ears show recent wounds, they have been beaten on their flanks. I think a report should be sent to the Department of Natural Resources as soon as possible so that a court order may be obtained to facilitate the rescue of these creatures.

In the town I have noted disquiet not only about the presence of the Romero Circus but with regard to the capture of these beasts for overtly commercial purposes. In the interviews I have been able to conduct, various local citizens consider the action of the Romero Circus an unpardonable affront carried out with the authorization of the mayor, Luis Bermúdez Santana.

I quote Dr. Onofre Bermúdez Rosario, owner of the Central Zorzal Pharmacy: "I have been in telephone contact with the congressman responsible for this senatorial district in order to inform him of my absolute rejection of the actions perpetrated in Centeno after the slaughter of various sagalús in the neighboring mountains and the capture of two of them. Their cries grieve us night after night.

I quote Municipal Assemblyman (Centeno) Ruperto Bermúdez Suárez: "I have presented to the Honorable Mayor Luis Bermúdez Santana a complaint co-signed by 35 of my fellow citizens concerning the invasion of Centeno by the Romero Circus, concerning the outrage perpetrated recently on numerous quadrupeds in the neighboring mountains and concerning the mistreatment of two of these animals in a circus tent set up in the Zorzal district of the municipality of Centeno."

I quote landowner Mrs. Elisa Gotay-Bermúdez: "I swear to you that in all of my 66 years of living here, I have never had to put up with such outrageous behavior. First, the outrage of the Romero Circus in setting up camp here; second, the outrage of tearing two of our poor deer from their mountain homes; third, and worst, the outrage of Mayor Bermúdez Santana for allowing these acts prejudicial to us to be perpetrated. I called the SPCA because to have remained silent would in itself have been criminal. I am happy you have come to attend to this complaint made by a retired schoolteacher who will not rest until justice is done in this town. As regards Mayor Bermúdez

Santana, I will make my objections to his capricious acts known to him in the upcoming elections."

I declare myself responsible for the veracity of this report. I thank the SPCA for this assignment, but I request that I be taken off the case for very urgent personal reasons.

He got up, lit another cigarette, and walked away from the disordered papers. He wanted to go back to Bayamón; he detested Ponce. He was divorced, with two children for whom he had, month after month, to pay child support. He felt alienated, especially now after being acceped at the University of Syracuse School of Veterinary Medicine, doubtless buried under snow. He wanted to get back as quickly as possible to Laura in Bayamón. He paced in front of the window, observing the couples strolling around the plaza and the measured steps of the parishioners on their way to seven o'clock mass. Ponce: God almighty!

He put the typewritten sheets in order and took out a few lines that disgusted him. After carefully folding them and placing them under the typewriter, he put out the lights and went out into the corridor putting the key in his pocket. He walked half a dozen steps, went back, and opened the door. Standing next to the typewriter, he ripped up the sheets and threw them into the wastepaper basket. Then he got on the elevator and headed for the bar.

Born in Puerto Rico in 1928, Pedro Juan Soto has published collections of short stories, several novels and theater pieces. This allegory reflects his feelings about the entrapment and elimination of potential dissidents. The story was translated by Alfred J. MacAdam.

"She shivered with the cold, and as the tiger
showed no signs of going away,
she grew desperate."

The Tiger

BY S. RAJARATNAM

FATIMA felt the cool yellow waters of the river—a sheet of
burnished gold in the dying sunglow—flow sluggishly around her.
She clung to the bank and moved further along until she stood
waist-deep in a shallower part of the river. The wet sarong clung to
her plump, brown figure and accentuated the full breasts and
womb of a pregnant woman. The round, high-cheekboned face, so
typical of the Malays, had been drained of its dark sensuality, and
instead an ethereal melancholy in the black oblique eyes gave her
the expression of one brooding over some pulsating vision within
herself.

With a quick toss of her head she unloosed her black, glossy
hair, and let the wind whisper gently through it. From where she
stood she could neither hear nor see the village obscured by the
creepers and trees at the bend of the river. In front of her stretched
an unbroken expanse of lalang grass, tall trees, and a bewildering
luxuriance of foliage. The languid stillness of the evening was

occasionally disturbed by the cry of a lonely water fowl, or the sinister flap, flap of night birds stirring from their sleep. Now and then a rat dived with a gentle splash into the river, while timid, nervous animals rustled their way through the tall grass and creepers. The air was full of the scent of wild flowers and mud and grass. A feeling of loneliness and desolation came over her, as though she had stumbled into a world still in the dawn of creation, when the earth was an oozing swamp in which wallowed a host of hideous monsters.

Hence when she heard the low, vibrant growl of the tiger it only heightened the illusion, until the tiger broke into a dull angry roar and convinced her that it was not a creature of her imagination.

Framed by the lalang and low to the ground were the massive head and shoulders of the tiger, not more than twenty yards from her. The sun imparted a wicked glint to its staring, yellow eyes, and its ears drawn back warningly. It turned its head and snarled, revealing its red tongue, and the yellow fangs looked like tree stumps.

Fatima was hypnotized into a helpless fear by the glaring eyes of the tiger, and the sudden stillness that fell around her numbed her mind. She dared not move or take her eyes away from the watching animal, which too was still as if it had been rendered motionless by the unexpected meeting with a human being.

Fatima and the animal watched one another, she frightened and it suspicious. Except for occasional growls, which became less menacing each time, the tiger showed no signs of really wanting to attack her. Instead, after a while the animal took a diminishing interest in her. Its huge paws, stretched out in front, now and then dug its claws into the damp grass. Except when she moved the animal's attention seemed to be nowhere in particular. The glare of its eyes had changed into a sullen and frequently bored expression, so that Fatima noticed the surprising changes of mood in the animal's eyes.

Meanwhile the dusk which had crept from over the hills had obliterated the colorful scene of a moment ago, and replaced it with gray shadows which drifted imperceptibly into darkness. A faint mist had risen from the river and had spread itself over the land. The shrill scream of a cicada and the distant hoot of an owl signaled the transition of the day into night.

Now that she had only a quiet fear of the tiger, she felt exhaustion creep over her. She shivered with cold, and as the tiger showed no signs of going away, she grew desperate. Her hands wandered over her stomach, and the realization that she was a being of two lives engendered in her a fierce determination to escape. She could still discern the shadowy form of the tiger by the failing light. Fatima had studied the animal very carefully and could sense when it would turn its eyes away from her. She waited, her body tense in the water and radiating a feeling of fearful strength. Then with a desperate movement she dived under water so that she scraped the riverbed as she swam. Fatima made for the opposite bank and in the direction of the village, coming to the surface only when she felt that her lungs would burst for air. She felt bewildered and lost in the middle of the river, but when she heard the faraway growl, a fear which she had not felt even in the presence of the tiger seized her.

She swam frantically towards the shore until she saw the twinkling oil lamps of the village.

The village was in a panic by the time Fatima's mother had spread an exaggerated version of the story her daughter had told her. The women, clucking like hens at the sight of a wheeling hawk, gathered the children into their arms, and having bolted their flimsy doors called out to the men to do something about the marauding tiger. The men rushed around, anxious about their cattle and goats, while the old men munched betel-nut and demanded what the fuss was all about.

Fatima lay exhausted on a straw mat when the village headman and a crowd came to question her as to the whereabouts of the tiger. Fatima's mother proceeded to give a graphic and noisy tale of her daughter's encounter with the "hairy one" until the headman, with an impatient gesture, commanded the old lady to hold her peace for a while. He then turned to question Fatima. There was impatience in her voice as she answered his questions. For some reason, unlike the anxious villagers around her, she was averse to having the tiger hunted and killed. The headman frowned.

"Allah!" exclaimed the old lady, wishing to be the center of interest once more. "It was the providence of Allah which snatched my daughter away from the jaws of the 'hairy one'."

She threw up her skinny brown hands in a gesture of thanks to Allah. The headman shrugged his shoulders.

"Perhaps it was," he said, "but the next time Allah will not be as merciful. A tiger, perhaps by now drunk with the scent of human flesh, is not a pleasant thing to have roving near our village. For the peace and safety of the women and children the beast must be hunted down and destroyed without delay."

He scanned the faces of the men, silent and nervous. They were fully alive to the dangers of tracking down a tiger at night, especially when the dense, shadowy lalang afforded it an advantageous position from which to strike quickly and silently.

"Well!" said the headman.

The men regarded the floor in silence. The headman's face twitched and he was about to upbraid them for their cowardice, when Mamood, his youthful face afire with excitement, came in with a gun slung across his shoulders.

"What is this I hear?" he asked eagerly. "The women told me that a tiger has attacked our Fatima. Is it true?"

While the headman told him the facts, briefly and accurately, Mamood fingered his new, double-barreled gun with all the impatience of one whose hunting spirit had been aroused. He was all for hunting the tiger at once, simply because he loved hunting. The fact that his quarry was a tiger made him all the more eager.

"That's true," said Mamood, when the headman had finished. "We have to think of the women and children. The poor creatures will never move an inch out of their houses until they know that the tiger is dead. It is the duty of the menfolk to protect them. Now who will come with Mamood and help him slay the tiger? As surely as I am the son of my mother I shall drag home the carcass of the beast before sunrise, if you will help me."

After some hesitation, a dozen men volunteered, encouraged by the words of Mamood and the knowledge that he was a good shot.

"Good!" exclaimed Mamood, running his fingers along the gun-barrel. "I knew I could rely on you."

Then he and the men left.

"Believe me, daughter," said Fatima's mother, as she bolted the door after the men, "that boy Mamood is a wild tiger himself."

Fatima rose up from her mat and looked out of the narrow window. The moon cast a mellow radiance over everything it touched, and she could see the moon, broken like molten silver, through the rustling coconut fronds. Men moved about calling out to one another in stifled, excited voices as they prepared for the hunt. Fatima stared sullenly at the men.

Then the men left until at last there was only the gray-garbed trees and the whisper of the fretful wind. Straining her ears she heard the faraway chuckle of the river.

Somewhere, she reflected, was the tiger about which she had wondered the whole evening. She hoped that it was far out of the men's reach.

"O Allah!" wailed her mother, pounding some areca-nut in a wooden vessel, "tonight is the night for death. Think of those men groping for a beast as cunning as a hundred foxes and which can measure its distance in the darkness. Sure enough there will be the cry of mourning before the night is over."

"They should have left the tiger alone," said Fatima, still looking out of the window.

"That's a crazy thing to say," said the woman. "Somebody has to kill the tiger before it kills us. That's sense."

"Perhaps it would have gone away of its own accord."

"A tiger which comes near a village does not go back until its purpose is accomplished," croaked the old woman. "They are generally killers which venture near a village."

"But this one didn't look like a killer," protested Fatima.

The old woman snorted contemptuously, but said nothing.

"The tiger was not more than twenty yards away from me and it could have sprung at me easily," said Fatima, "but it didn't. Why? Can you explain that, Mother? It kept watching me, it's true, but then I was watching it too. At first its eyes glared at me, but later they were gentle and bored. There was nothing fierce or murderous about it..."

"Now you are talking the crazy way your father used to," said her mother fiercely pounding the areca-nut. "He used to say that the wind sang songs to him. Heaven forgive me that I should talk so of your dead father, but he was a crazy man sometimes."

Fatima scowled out of the window and listened. There was an unearthly silence over the village as though enveloped in a funeral shroud. Her hands, swollen and fleshy, were clenched tightly as she strained the silence for some revealing sound. The pound, pound of her heart kept pace with the jabs her mother made into the areca-nut vessel. Then a sharp pain shot through her. Her hands went over her stomach.

"What is it, Fatima?" said her mother looking up.

"Nothing," answered Fatima between pressed lips.

"Come away from that draught and lie down," cautioned her mother.

Fatima stood by the window and felt the pain rise and fall. She closed her eyes and pictured the tiger crouching in the lalang, its eyes now red and glaring, now bored and gentle.

Then she heard the faraway crack of a rifle. Then another shot followed. Fatima quivered as if the shots had been aimed at her. Then came the roar of the tiger; not the mild growl she had heard that evening, but full of pain and defiance. For a few seconds the cry of the animal, long drawn out in its agony, seemed to fill up her heart and ears. She wanted to re-echo the cry. Her face was tight with pain and her body glistened with sweat. A moan broke between her shut lips.

"Allamah! Allamah!" cried out the old woman. "You look ill. What is it? Come and lie down. Is it...?"

"I've got the pains, Mother," gasped Fatima.

The old woman led the girl towards the mat and made her lie down.

"Oi, oi, it's a fine time to have a baby!" cried her mother, a little frightened. "You lie down here while I get you some hot water to drink. I'll have to wait till the men return before I go for the midwife. Ay, this is a fine night for a poor old woman!"

Fatima lay on the mat, her eyes shut tight while her mother

boiled the water and muttered.

"Listen," said the old woman, "the men are returning. I can hear their voices."

The air suddenly was filled with the excited voices of men and women outside.

The old lady opened the door cautiously and called out to someone.

"Hurrah for Mamood, Auntie," cried a youth rushing in. "He's shot the tiger and they have dragged the beast home. It's a big animal. No wonder it put up a good fight before it was killed. After it was shot twice they had to spear it before it was really killed. And then what do you think happened?"

Fatima looked attentively at the youth. The old lady turned her tiny shriveled head impatiently towards the youth.

"Well, what happened?"

"They said," explained the youth, lisping slightly, "that after they had killed the animal they heard noises. Then by the light of the hurricane lamps they saw three of the tiniest tiger-cubs. Their eyes were scarcely open and Mamood says that they could not be more than a few hours old. No wonder the beast fought like one possessed. Mamood says that he could sell the tiger-cubs for a good price."

Fatima moaned in pain. The sweat glistened like yellow pearls on her forehead.

"Mother!" she cried.

The old woman pushed the astonished youth towards the door.

"Get the midwife, boy," she shouted. "Quick! Go! The midwife." The youth stared, gasped and then ran for the midwife.

A remarkably talented short story writer, S. Rajaratnam has also served Singapore as Foreign Minister. His short stories are included in anthologies and published in the UK, USA and Australia.

"You'll change your mind. Don't forget you can never be happy outside your native land."

Alien Corn

BY JOSEPH PATRON

WHEN they found the farm, round midday, it turned out to be halfway up a mountain on a broad ledge of land covered with tall ripe corn. It was a sprawling stone building with a raised passageway round it and a projecting wooden roof. Some steps led down from the front entrance, with a weatherbeaten wooden statue on the lintel, to a clearing covered with farming implements and steaming heaps of manure. The smell of freshly turned earth mingled with that of loose chaff. In the dark shade of a fig tree an old woman sat nursing a baby. A peace reigned there that seemed never to have known the World War which had ended less than a year before.

As the nose of the jeep with Lieutenant Martin at the wheel entered the clearing, the old woman rose and moved away behind some shrubs. A sullen, burly man in leather shorts emerged from the porch on the top steps and asked Martin gruffly in German, or Austrian, who they were and what they wanted. Martin said he was a British officer accompanying a Soviet Mission for Repatriation and that the Soviet Colonel would explain the purpose of their visit.

In the meantime the Mercedes had come to a halt and the Soviet group was approaching. Colonel Savneke made his way forward and announced in his shaky German: "We are the Soviet Mission for Repatriation. We believe there is a Ukrainian girl here. We wish to speak to her."

Unperturbed, sucking at his curved pipe, the farmer muttered "Grüss Gott" and strode heavily down the steps. In a relaxed manner he said, "There's no Russian girl here."

Martin had only recently arrived in Austria, fresh from his short Army Russian course, but he was already familiar with some of the local tensions and could see that the farmer resented the Colonel's peremptory tone.

The three Soviet officers and the N.C.O., Galanin, with the red band on his cap, began to whisper among themselves. The place corresponded to the description they had been given in Lientz, the small town in the Ost Tirel where they were temporarily lodged.

The Colonel turned to say that the girl's name was Nadezhada Gabrilienka. The farmer shrugged his shoulders. Martin beckoned to the Austrian and some paces away explained that the Soviets wanted to see the girl to find out if she wished to return to the Ukraine, and that since this was part of the British Zone, he was there to see that her wishes were respected. The farmer hesitated, then said in a low voice: "Wir ha'm 'n Mad'l hier. We have a girl here. She's worked on our farm for four years. She wants to stay. If you like I can call her, but she may be frightened." Martin nodded to the Soviets and they trooped round the farmhouse and out towards the cornfields.

Early that morning, on leaving Lientz, the sky had promised a clear, spring day but as they climbed, the clouds had built up over the skyline. Now the horizon that faced them threatened rain. A single patch of blue shone overhead like a watchful eye.

The Colonel went ahead beside the farmer, tramping over the hard cart-ruts, his trim figure erect, his calf-high riding boots as yet undirtied by the mud. He had Mongolian features, a small, round face with wide cheekbones and narrow, blue-gray eyes. His skin was a lacquered yellow, his hair close-cropped and graying. The inner white strip that showed above his collar accentuated his military cut. He was a man of action but, as Martin knew, of reflection also.

The previous evening Martin had had an interesting conversation with him. In the room of the stout Austrian medical student who occupied one of the wooden shacks in the *Lazarett,* or hospital, where they had temporary living quarters, Martin had come across a book, in English, on atomic energy (this was not long after Hiróshima and Nagasaki) and he took it with him on his visit to the Colonel to work out the day's program.

The Colonel was sitting at a table in the center of their large common room so as to get the light from the single bare bulb. His gray head was bowed over one of the long lists of names they had received from their Intelligence Service in Vienna. Beside the list was a pamphlet: *The Motherland Needs You.* Martin was familiar with its contents. It was an appeal to patriotism: Russian patriotism disguised as Soviet patriotism. It said the Soviet Government reached out for her lost children like a loving mother. It was new and strange to Martin, this personified relationship, this methodical persistence in the search for *its own,* even when they weren't in any special need or danger. He had read during his Russian course at Cambridge that in the remote past, too, from the time of the State of Muscovy, Russia had hunted down its citizens the same way, as if they were *owned* by the Tsar.

The Colonel looked up.

"Tomorrow we're going into the country. Unfortunately, both our cars are in the workshop. They may not be ready in time. But we've got the jeep. We want to see a girl who works on a farm. I can't understand why they don't stay in the camps provided for them instead of wandering off into the countryside. It makes our task so much harder. We heard she came to Lientz to make inquiries about repatriation, but the office was closed."

Galanin, the N.C.O., was standing against the wall, his elbows resting back on the high window sill, his tunic conspicuously undone at the neck, his cap pushed back, revealing his bristly round head. It was unusual for him, this informal stance. He had not been expecting Martin's entry into the room. Beside him, Lieutenant Spirin yawned, perusing a yellowed copy of *Pravda.* But on seeing Galanin button up his tunic and walk towards the door, he put down the newspaper and followed him out of the room.

"If the cars are ready, we'll make a day of it," the Colonel continued, "otherwise we'll go on with the registration in town. We can't all fit into the jeep."

Martin suggested they use his Mercedes. But, as usual, when he was obliged to employ one of Martin's vehicles, the Colonel didn't like to accept the offer openly. He just nodded as if the matter were settled and continued with his own line of thought.

Martin knew the Colonel was just then seriously concerned about the feelings of resentment towards the Mission on the part of the locals. There had even been talk of depriving them of their office in town because of the posters they had put up. The Colonel, though, was better informed than Martin about all this. He was certainly aware that in June the year before about 130 Soviet troops had committed suicide in the area of Lientz in the Ost Tirol rather than be repatriated to their country. In fact throughout Austria, in that idyllic natural setting, there had been many Red Army deserters and P.O.W.s who had chosen to kill themselves rather than return to the USSR. And at this time, in 1946, there were Austrians in Lientz who recalled seeing the remnants of Cossack units being rounded up after they had abandoned the main body of the Red Army. Memories were still fresh; these things had occurred only a year before; and this caused the ill-feeling that worried the Colonel.

Even without this, though, the Colonel always had plenty to grumble about in his conversations with Martin. He accused the Western Allied powers, and the Austrians, of hindering their work. In fact, as Martin knew, it was not easy to know where to draw the line sometimes in these matters of repatriation. The Treaty of Yalta had, perhaps inadvertently, left certain things vague. Also, from the time of their arrival in Lientz the Colonel had shown his distress at the bareness of the quarters where they were billeted. Martin had gone on ahead from Klagenfurt (the main town in the southernmost province of Austria, Carinthia, bordering on Yugoslavia, where they were stationed) to see about lodgings and rations, and to find a suitable office for the Mission's work. In the town the streets were deserted. It was cold, and the only lodgings he found, two wooden bungalows or shacks in the pre-fabricated *Lazarett,* were poorly heated.

For the first few days they subsisted on meager rations they had sent on from Klagenfurt. Then, when Martin found out that there were British troops quartered in this area, the food was delivered every few days by the garrison's catering officer. One day they failed to arrive and their breakfast consisted of hunks of dry bread. The British catering officer had married an Austrian girl whose parents had been shot by the Soviets and he was not over-eager to satisfy the Mission's requirements. Then the British Garrison was posted elsewhere, so that for lack of provisions the Mission had to cut short its stay in this area from the intended two weeks.

The offices for the Mission's work that Martin had found consisted of three small rooms in the center of town. The value of the place was for the most part symbolic. At no time did Martin see more than one or two timid, shoddily dressed individuals drop in, either out of curiosity to peruse the printed material laid out on the tables, or in answer to a summons for questioning. The poster outside the office, like the one at the Townhall, simply stated that the Soviet Mission was in town and that anyone could freely avail himself of the opportunity. But these and other posters were repeatedly torn down, until they were *left* down. Nowhere else in the British Zone did Martin encounter such dumb, but active, hostility to the Mission. At one camp they were surrounded by angry refugees, shouted at and stoned; and Martin, who tended to be identified with the Mission's work, found himself hard put to calm down the crowd.

The Soviets knew that in Lientz the D.P.s they were looking for were scattered in the neighborhood, mostly in the countryside working for Austrian farmers. So they concentrated on the records in the Townhall and the oral reports they gathered from a few locals. Also, it was known that early White Russians were particularly numerous in this part of Austria, and these expressed their antipathy whenever they could. In Lientz there was a Center founded by a White Russian woman. One day the Soviets turned up uninvited, hoping to discover secret hideouts for D.P.s in its walls. But they were disappointed. There were no Soviet D.P.s. Everywhere they found an atmosphere of industry and peace. The White Russians knew when, and how, to be diplomatic.

In the common room in the *Lazarett,* the Colonel stared at the book on atomic energy which Martin had placed on the table. Printed matter had a peculiar, potentially subversive, fascination for them. Taking the book in his hands and spelling out the English title, the Colonel turned to the front pages, fingering them with respect.

"I, too, am a student of energy," he said. Martin sat beside him scanning the front page of *Pravda.* It had a characteristic odor: a mixture of cheap ink and sawdust. Straddled across the page was a faded photo of the review stand over the Lenin Mausoleum, like a Sumerian Ziguratt, lined with heavily coated, sour-faced commissars.

The Colonel asked the meaning of the caption under an algebraic formula. Martin excused himself for not knowing the Russian equivalent of the technical mathematical terms. In any case he did not know what they represented, so he could not convey their meaning.

With a pensive air, the Colonel went carefully—with pointed finger—through the index. Finally, he handed the book back saying, "My English is not good enough."

Later, with a mock-serious smile, over a glass of brandy, he told Martin about his own philosophical views: a mixture of modern scientific theory and Buddhism, a semi-religious "evolutionism." Before they parted he remarked enigmatically, stroking the linen under his tight-fitting mandarin collar, that he was descended from the Emperor of Japan. With the tone of his voice he deliberately put this statement on a level with his philosophic views, so that Martin, by then under the influence of the brandy, could no longer tell what the Colonel's real opinions might be. One thing was certain: he was no orthodox Marxist.

Now, at the mountain farm, as Martin watched him hurrying beside the farmer along the dirt path towards the cornfields, with his parchment-colored complexion and short neat figure, trying to keep ahead of the others (he must have been over sixty but he looked less), it seemed to Martin that the possibility of his aristocratic, or even divine, descent (the Emperor of Japan was held to be the son of god) should not be discounted.

The far border of the field sloped sharply away so that the harvester, the two men and the girl, half-hidden in the corn, were silhouetted against the darkening horizon. The farmer called out to the girl as she drew near, but not by her Ukrainian name. She was close to the harvester and half-turned in their direction, holding the kerchief in one hand—like Ruth, thought Martin, "amid the alien corn." She was heavily built but not fat and wore a plain, flower-patterned frock. As she stepped onto the path, she removed her headscarf, revealing thick blond hair that fell in curls to her shoulders. Her cheeks were flushed as she looked up, unabashed, at the Soviet officers.

For the sake of formality, the Colonel asked if her name was Nadezhda Gabrilienka. She bowed her head in assent and before the Colonel could ask another question, added that nobody called her that now.

"We were told you wanted to see us about returning to your native land (*rodina*)," he said.

The others drew closer, standing round the girl.

"If you like," said the Colonel, "you can come with us now. Do you want to come now?"

She looked down. "I don't know."

The Colonel lowered his voice to a whisper. "You'd be happier there. Your country needs you. It's your duty to return to where you belong." He might have been quoting verbatim from one of his brochures, and he probably was. He had a wad of brochures in his pocket.

With her eyes still averted, the girl said impetuously: "I know about those camps where they shoot you if you don't obey or if you're too weak to move. And when you arrive they keep you in

119

quarantine for two years...in a separate camp...for indoctrination."

She was controlling herself as she spoke, but when the members of the Mission began to talk among themselves and the Colonel turned to her again, raising his voice, she put a handkerchief to her eyes and began to sob.

The farmer had been giving her moral support, nodding as she spoke. Now, as her tears flowed faster, he held her by the elbow and spoke in her ear. And just when it seemed she was no longer listening, to their surprise, she looked up, her eyes like a child's glazed with tears, and rubbing her cheeks dry, muttered, "And they give you only watery soup..."

The Soviets moved restlessly about, embarrassed by this sustained display of emotion. Galanin leaned towards the Colonel and made a gesture of impatience.

The farmer said to Martin, "She's fond of a Yugoslav. They met here working in the fields and she wants to stay with him."

Then the girl spoke once again, huskily, her clenched fist with the wet handkerchief to her breast. "They make you sleep on wooden planks...everyone knows about it..."

The Soviet officers prepared to leave. Martin told the Colonel what the farmer had said and saw his face darken as he said he wanted to see the young man. The farmer answered that he was working nearby collecting stones. He would go and fetch him. He raised his eyes to the girl, then to Martin, and ambled off, puffing vigourously at his pipe.

The two workers who had remained standing by the harvester now approached as if to take the place of the farmer and stood conversing close to the girl. Martin looked at the girl, now that she was no longer under the constant scrutiny of the Colonel. Though he would have found it difficult to formulate with any clarity, or at all, his own inner conflicts, he felt that there was much in his own situation that was reflected in her predicament. At that moment she symbolized so well what his work was all about, and even something deeper. He too was young, under pressure from large events, obscure motivations. But whereas with the Soviet Mission, and especially in the presence of the Colonel, he was virtually just a nuisance, raw, ill-informed, and pretentious in his interpretation of the decisions taken at Yalta, she—by contrast—seemed to be in place in the colorful beauty of the Austrian countryside: domesticated yet somehow wild, hemmed in by foreign armies, yet in her element, at peace.

Some days before, Martin had seen a party of fair-haired young women like her, only more carefree, singing to the accompaniment of a mouth-organ. From the *Lazarett* he had gone by jeep with the medical student, who was roughly his own age, to see the Gross Gleckner, the highest peak in the area, some twenty miles north of Lientz. All afternoon they sat, the student in leather shorts, with the glacier below and the valley filled with sun. It was the student's first view of the Gleckner since his childhood before the war. Now, in the clear light of spring, he was awed by the grandeur of the scene. The Gleckner was visible down to its shadowed base, with the glacier with its huge cracks and rifts. Near the highest peak three specks that were human beings moved imperceptibly. The student said that climbing at this time of year was not allowed without a guide because of the danger of landslides.

Below them was the immense valley, cut in two by the river which shone like mercury in a limp Deli thermometer. It was only distinguishable from the gleaming main roads by the irregularity and length of its course. They seemed to have left below them a great layer of sunshine, fixed in a timeless moment, resting on hamlets and hedges and on the barely visible pinpoints of cattle in the pastures. When every now and then the student, out of sheer exuberance, burst out into snatches of yodeling song, the trilling sound carried across the valley. And once, as if in answer, there echoed from below, the strains of Brahm's *Serenade.* How this tranquility contrasted, thought Martin, with the task of the Mission at the *Lazarett,* with the pursuit of helpless D.P.s, some of whom had at last found at least the promise of a new life and had no wish to leave.

There were deep evening shadows on the mountainside as they descended the steep, stony track, stopping to pick *alpen rosen* and blue gentians. They walked with a sense of contentment, as if they had just interviewed some great man whose words of departure had filled them with happiness. Up above they could still catch glimpses of the summit of the Gleckner, paper-white against the sky.

At the *Gasthaus,* where an enterprising British Mayor ran a skiing school in the winter months, groups of people sat at long tables sipping the colored water which passed for lemonade in the aftermath of war. Among them in the courtyard were Americans with expensive cameras and Frenchmen in berets.

The rest of the journey by jeep down into the valley they took little notice of the woods, clearings, and wooden chalets with their dark brown roofs and geranium-filled balconies. As they reached the lowlands, the student once more lapsed into a pensive, melancholy mood. He spoke to Martin in tragic tones of his people and the fate that surely awaited them. He was convinced that before long the land would be overrun by Soviet tanks.

When they stopped to visit a diminutive mountain chapel, a horsecart passed by with youngsters singing Schubert's *Guten Abend, Gute Nacht,* and in the music the beauty and sadness of the occasion seemed to merge together.

At the mountain farm, as the young Yugoslav and the farmer drew near, the atmosphere was more tense. Over the harvester, long clouds, like marble steps worn and rounded by the trample of gigantic feet, lay one on another. Colonel Savenke had almost decided to cut short the interrogation. The Yugoslav was dressed in an open check shirt and what looked like British K.D. trousers. His face and arms were a dark brown from work in the fields. He stopped a few paces away and stared fixedly at the Colonel.

"This is Ivan," said the farmer. "He already knows what you want and says it's up to her to decide."

The old woman with the baby came up from behind the Yugoslav and stood by the girl, forming a group with the farmer and the workmen, as if weighing the scales in favor of the girl's staying.

The Colonel was examining the new arrival. He seemed now to regret that he had summoned him. It would have been simpler without him. Emotions complicate and weaken the black and white categories of the ideological, or even semi-ideological, cast of mind. There was always Galanin's presence that the Colonel needed to take into account.

In a final effort at conciliation, he said to the girl: "However well you've been treated here, you're still among strangers." He glanced at the Yugoslav, noting his reactions to his words. "These are not your people. When you get back you'll be sent to your relatives. What you said about the way you'd be treated, is nothing but anti-Soviet slander."

The Yugoslav glared back and made a move as if to intervene.

"There'll be many Ukrainian young men to take the place of your friend," muttered the Colonel.

He had tried, crudely, to allay her fears. But now Martin could see they had reached an impasse. An ominous drop of rain fell on the stony earth between the two groups and they raised their heads. The farmer motioned the two workmen to return to the harvester. The Colonel produced a sheaf of leaflets from his pocket and thrust them under his arm to protect them from the rain. It was clear by the way he was ready to have recourse to the printed material, that he thought spoken words were of no further avail. As he gave the girl a last look of appraisal, wondering if he should make a final attempt to shake her resolution, she forestalled him. Leaning on the old woman's shoulder, she said with a quick look at the Yugoslav, but loud so they could all hear: *"I want to stay with him."*

The Colonel stared at the young couple. "He could come too," he said after a pause, "or he could follow after." But with this his patience came to an end. As he turned to leave he said, "You'll change your mind. Don't forget you can never be happy outside your native land."

In Martin's view, the Colonel's attitude had gone beyond simple persuasion. This was tantamount to moral coercion. He had been on the point of intervening: it was his job. What held him back was the fact that the Soviet officer had by now clearly lost his customary air of aloof superiority. He had pushed things too far. He had bungled it. He was confronted by people—of three nationalities—who were agreed among themselves; the more the encounter was prolonged, the more their conviction hardened. The

Colonel had been torn between trying to interpret the girl's feelings and reactions, and his concern with the impression he was making on the other members of the Mission. The presence of the young British Lieutenant hardly worried him. Being better informed about decisions taken by the Allied Commanders at a higher, or at the highest, level, he knew how far he could go. But he didn't want to appear weak before his junior officers or the ever-watchful Galanin. They knew that as their Commanding Officer, he was not one to back out easily. But now he looked tired and pale through his parchment-colored skin. To Martin his claim to divine descent now seemed much less plausible.

It had started to rain. The girl and the Yugoslav stood together, hand in hand, like a pair of runaway children. How little it takes to decide a person's destiny! Galanin ran back to the car. The patch of blue still shone overhead, but now it was a long, wavering streak, like the last pennant on a field of battle, while the rest of the sky swirled with shapeless black masses. As if marking the conclusion of the encounter, the churning sound of the harvester had ceased. The Colonel went up to the girl and pushed a handful of propaganda leaflets into her hands. Taken by surprise, she stepped back so that the leaflets were scatttered in the mud at her feet.

No one moved to collect them. The Colonel stared down, glancing at his mud-covered boots, and then angrily at the Yugoslav who seemed to him to be responsible for all this. Often it happened that way: the unpredictable factor turned out to be the decisive one. It was a lesson that Galanin—who was ideologically trained, and through whose political conscience the Colonial acted, at any rate when in his presence—had not yet adequately learned.

The N.C.O. was already at the wheel of the Mercedes, trying to start up, with the officers climbing in at the back, when he saw the leaflets spattered on the muddy ground. At once he left the car and rushed to pick them up conscientiously one by one. He knew the value of printed matter.

"Give her time to think it over," the Colonel repeated to the farmer. "She needs time to think it over."

The girl, the elderly woman and the farmer moved slowly in the direction of the house, looking round every now and then, but hoping to reach cover before the downpour. Only the Yugoslav remained motionless on the verge of the cornfield, his face set, his fists clenched, as if his immobility was a condition of their leaving.

Colonel Savenke climbed in the front seat of the Mercedes beside Galanin and with a gesture of his arm shouted in Slavic German through the rain and the noise of the engine, "We'll be back!"

In the jeep Martin pressed the clutch and got into gear. This time he knew they wouldn't.

J.F. Patron, a resident of Spain, was born in Gibraltar in 1925. He has a Ph.D. from Oxford (Trinity College), speaks French, Russian, Italian, Spanish and English, and is widely traveled. Dr. Patron has taught on the college level in the U.S.A. and Italy and been associated with publishers in England, Italy and the U.S.A. His articles, poems and stories are published mainly in England; his travel books have been published in Italian translation.

"Your problem is you don't respect anyone
or anything except yourself."

Big Dog

BY NORMAN LAVERS

SHE of course wanted the old villa about five miles out of town,
surrounded by lantana and bougainvillaea, with its quaint patio and
tile roof through which, in places, you could see the metallic blue
Mediterranean sky. He looked at the plumbing, the improvised
electric wiring, the inconvenient distance from the shops—"We'll
have our bikes," she said. "Winter, wet and rainy, is coming even
here," he said—and gave a decisive negative. He wanted the brand
new apartment on the fourth floor in the middle of town,
everything working, right in the center of things. She saw the
sterile functionalism, the cool anonymous neighbors, the lack of
anything alive and growing, and in her own passive way dug in her
heels. She apologetically asked, he abruptly demanded, that the
real estate agent show them something else, and they
compromised on an older, more lived-in apartment on the edge of
town with fields and a lagoon to look at off their balcony, which
was only one floor up from the ground. Also, they were childless,
and she had noticed a frail elderly couple in the little house next

door. Her curiously inverted maternal instinct always needed old people to protect and preserve.

He for his part—well—he didn't know what he was going to do, only that, when he found it, he would rush at it head first, and it would not long resist him. Some people in this world are dreamers, sleeping light and dreaming through the night, half awake by day, their dreams rushing in at every odd moment. For such people— she was a bit like this—the place is only partly important, because so much of their life goes on independently from place. He was the other way, constantly fully alert, taking in everything, obsessively seeing and learning every process around him at the top of his speed, putting all of himself into it. But it had to be the *it* that was objectively out there, and when it was not there for him, and his interest flagged, he was deeply asleep in a moment, his face sagging, his mouth drooped open. In this way he was like those sharks who must swim constantly their whole life, because if they pause, the oxygen is no longer carried past their breathing apparatus, and they die.

But the doctor had ordered him to rest, and he had taken the long overdue sabbatical. He meant to rest, however, one hundred percent. He laid out the campaign in his head. He had first of all quit smoking cold turkey, and after reading every book, had set up a balanced diet for himself that would work off his extra sixty pounds. He would go down to the beach and do distance swimming in the morning as long as the weather stayed warm—it was already the end of September—and he had bought a knife-thin racing bike for distance biking in the afternoon till he had lost his extra weight, at which time the doctor told him he could begin running. Right now the weight would be too much strain on his knees.

On the day they looked at their apartment, clouds covered the distant view. But on the day they moved into it from their hotel it was clear. They did their grocery shopping, haltingly in the unfamiliar language—and she made them their first pot of tea, and they sat out on their balcony, and at that point for the first time realized that it was the mountain that would dominate their view. It was Puig Major, rising 6000 feet straight up out of the sea. In the local island dialect Puig was pronounced like Pooch, so he dubbed the mountain Big Dog. It was a bare pinnacle of rock. She decided it was a volcanic spewing, magma pressing up from the dark middle of the world. He saw in it another—to him even more dramatic—orogenetic force, the great African plate pressing north into the Eurasian plate, pushing and squeezing up the land between this wrinkle which went from the Atlas Mountains in Morocco the length of the western Mediterranean at last curving northward and culminating in the Alps.

"What are you going to do?" he said.

"For the rest of my life?" she said. "For this year? Or just this morning?"

"Those three in that order?"

"I'm just going to go on puttering for my life. For this year I want to do some different kind of painting, but I don't know what yet. And for this morning I'm going to lie on the beach with my new bikini. I'll be the one you don't notice because I'll still have my top on. You're going to lie on the beach and take it easy on your heart."

"My heart is okay."

"Now. But you're in the number one risk category."

"Yeah, well there's another side to that equation. More and more evidence is coming in that there is also a number one risk cancer personality, and that's marked by people who are too passive."

"I'm not too passive."

"Only because I keep agitating you."

"Well, if I keep pulling you back, it's for your own good."

"Hey, stop pushing me around," he said, smiling and she smiled too, both because it was so unusual for her to be assertive in anything, and because on the face of it the idea was so ludicrous. She had never weighed over ninety pounds. He wasn't tall, but he was broad as a door, and had gone to university on football scholarships till he got a head injury and began passing out. Then to the amazement of his jock friends, he went on and made it through academically, even through the Ph.D., and taught in a university with surprising brilliance. He took his first chance to move to a department chairmanship, and then to a Dean of Arts and Sciences position. No matter where he was, he systematically set about learning his and everyone else's job, then began working on ways to improve them, and by the time he had made himself indispensable, was beginning to get bored.

They were funny to see together on the beach. She was like his child with her tiny perfect body. When he put suntan lotion on her, one of his hands could cover her whole back. His stomach was big, but his chest was massive.

"I'm going for a swim."

"I'm going to lie here and soak up the sun."

He marched out into the sea up to his knees. At the farthest end of the harbor, two or three miles away, was the last out ship channel marker. He dove in with an immense splash and struck out towards it. He was so buoyant he seemed to wallow at the surface, rolling from side to side with his formless but powerful crawl stroke. He did not let up his pace till he reached the marker. There, he held on for a few minutes, breathing hard, and waited, but nothing struck his heart. He swam back at a somewhat more leisurely pace, and walked out onto the beach, water streaming off his shaggy body, his muscles pumped up to even more herculean proportions.

He lay down next to her and watched the topless bathers for a while, then watched all the people on the beach one after the other, trying to guess about their lives from what they looked like. He watched the windsurfers for a while, but that didn't seem very challenging.

"I can't stand lying here doing nothing," he said.

They went back to the apartment and had lunch and she went on sunbathing on the balcony, this time with no bikini. He liked that and watched her for a while, and then they made love. Once when they were staying with friends they had been making love in the guest bedroom when they realized there was a long mirror beside the bed. They looked over and saw the huge hairy monster with the tiny fragile child engulfed under him, and they both laughed so hard they had to stop what they were doing. But luckily for the most part they made love with their eyes closed, and it was the one thing he did gently, and she did fiercely.

When he stood up, the mountain was there in his view. He rode his bike up as high as the road went, chained it to a tree, and climbed to the top of the mountain. He looked around and saw water on all sides. "So much for that," he said, and was back at the flat in time to fix a drink before dinner.

"This island might start getting a bit small," he said. And while she watched him, his attention lapsed, and his eyes lost focus, and his face sagged in the direction of gravity. It was the end of their first day in the apartment.

However, he threw himself into his study of the language. He was fascinated to see how logical it was, how efficient. How by merely changing *a* to *e* in the verb paradigms they could be made to reflect action from a different perspective. He would study a particular point of grammar all morning, wandering around the house muttering, then in the afternoon he would walk downtown and try to talk to a newsagent, to a shopkeeper, working everything they said around so that he could use that particular point of grammar. He bought a tiny tape recorder which he kept in his pocket where it couldn't be seen, and recorded conversations, then played them over and over again when he got back to the apartment, analyzing them. He saw the ad, taped to a shop window, for a group of language tutors, and hired one to come by every morning for an hour class.

She in the meantime in her very quiet way slowly put her stamp on their living space. She filled the balcony and every empty spot with pots of growing plants. The rather standardized furnishings in their furnished apartment seemed as if they would resist personalization, but with the tiniest shifts—the equivalent of changing *a* to *e*—she turned each area into something recognizably her own. Each meal she fixed was individual and beautiful to look at, the local food and dishes given a slightly oriental quality. She had gone to Japan one summer to study painting and was delighted to find a whole country just her size, and designed and organized the way she designed and organized a meal or a room. She had studied Japanese for several months before going over, and he told her it was the perfect language for her, as it seemed to consist of dozens of ways of apologizing for your presence.

He was not by any means blind to the small and perfect beauty always surrounding her, and that he himself sat in somewhat jarringly, but no longer uneasily. He liked it. Maybe she could extend her subtle power to him, and make him, within her magic circle, somewhat less gross and incongruous. She seemed to think it was no problem.

"You mean strength matters too, not just beauty."

"Not exactly," she said. "I mean they're not different. My painting master showed me a very old painting. There were three figures. Quite intentionally, I'm sure, there was no attempt to make the composition interesting. It was just three forms, all the same size, placed equidistant across the board they were painted on. One was a peony, traditionally epitomizing beauty, but that only lasts for a day. The next was a lion, incredible strength and fearlessness and vitality. The third was a rock, perdurable, resistless, eternal."

"And they all belonged in the same painting."

"More than that. They were all the same shape. If you squinted your eyes slightly—"

"So you would see them as an oriental would."

"Yes, I hadn't thought of that—you would see that the stone really looked very much like the peony, the peony like the lion, and so on. That what was perfect in the flower was enduring, that what was beautiful in the stone was transitory, that the lion's strength was as fragile, his courage as perfect—you could probably say this all better than I can."

"No. I think I understand," he said. It was her he couldn't fathom. She was the one process he couldn't analyze, had given up trying to, which is why perhaps he never grew bored with her.

He thought he had dismissed the mountain after the first day, and yet as he paced through the apartment muttering hypothetical conversations, at the end of his pace he was always on the balcony looking at Big Dog.

"It's never the same twice," he said.

"Have you just noticed that?" she said.

Now he also noticed what she was doing. She had taken out a

large sheet of watercolor paper and with a pencil and a straight-edge was lightly platting it out in 2-1/2 inch squares. He sat and watched her. She fumbled hesitatingly through her life, but when she worked she was almost grimly efficient. Now she took an ordinary sheet of paper and cut a 2-1/2 inch square out of the middle of it and held it at arm's length before her, and looked at the mountain through it. With her other hand she did drawings of the mountain, and when she had one that pleased her, she traced it on her tracing paper. Then she turned her tracing paper over and blacked the backside with a soft pencil. She turned the paper face up again and placed it over the first of the squares on her big sheet of watercolor paper, and with a hard pencil went over the lines of her original drawing, so that the carbon underneath transferred the line to the watercolor paper. Slowly and carefully she repeated this over each square.

He began taking an interest in the process. "You know there is such a thing as carbon paper, that would do the job a lot quicker and easier."

She ignored him.

"What you're going to do now is paint it every time it changes, right?"

"Mm-hmm."

"Now's the time to start," he said, beginning to take over. "There's a neat lenticular cloud forming over the peak. Here, I'll set up a chair and table for you."

"I have to fix your lunch right at the moment."

"That can wait. This is more important. It's already shifting."

But she went in and began preparing lunch. Partly, she was resisting having him take over. She could be as stubborn as he was. More so. In her soft but persistent way she could wear him down as water does stone. He knew this and felt helpless now, wishing he had not said anything. He had not meant to take over her idea, it's just that it had seemed like such a good idea to him, and he was already anticipating the pleasure he would have in seeing the mountain captured in each new view. He told himself not to say another word, otherwise she would not do it at all. Even as he looked, the lens cloud was lifting and losing its shape, and before he sat down to lunch it was gone forever.

In the morning when he opened his eyes, it immediately came to mind, and though he would like to have lain there holding her small intensely warm body, he got up and rushed to the balcony. After a night of high winds—the stormy season was fast approaching—the air was absolutely clear. The mountain seemed much closer, and the slant light gouged a deep black shadow across part of the front. The hard rock glowed in the sun.

"You should see it now," he said eagerly, going back to the bed. "It's the absolutely primal rock right now, no atmospheric effects, simply what is there, the bare bones." He said it as temptingly as possible, barely restraining himself from saying, "This is the time to start." She was not buying, however. She wanted something else for the moment and reached her arms up to him.

When he got up the second time a bank of cloud as solid as whipped cream was pushing up against one side of the mountain, and puffy clouds were appearing in a line above the horizon. He stopped himself from remarking on it, but she read his eyes perhaps. She went into the kitchen and began preparing their breakfast.

While they ate breakfast, the space between Big Dog and two smaller closer mountains filled in with solid cloud or fog, and a high overcast crept over the sky subduing the light, except for a point of sun still illuminating the peak, as if at the end of a gloomy tunnel. Then the overcast thickened, and the light on the mountain failed, and it was only a dull gray outline. The cloud system moved rapidly, clearing from behind them, and soon the sky was clear overhead, and sun covered the land, leaving only the mountain in a swirling gloom. He was in agony watching the changes, each ideally illustrative of a new facet of the mountain's personality, and each quickly lost. In the meantime she had gone out to do the shopping.

In the evening it went through all the same or similar changes in reverse, only this time everything bathed in fire, until at last the mountain, clear again, was stark and black against a sky like a thin sheet of molten steel slowly cooling and darkening. They sat long over their after-dinner coffees watching until the last spark was extinguished.

In the middle of the night he got up and came to look at it. The clouds had built up again and all outside was intensely purple black, except where reddish lightning flickered about the peak as if around the head of some monster about to be brought to life. He went back to the bed, aching to tell her, to get her to see it, but she was breathing easily, fast asleep.

The next day, she packed lunch and a thermos for him which he put in his backpack, and he took off on his bike heading for a town 25 miles down the coast, on the other side of the mountain, where he would have a different view of it. The wind had shifted direction and was coming from the mountain, and thunderheads were building behind it. He didn't bother to take a raincoat. He only had on a tee-shirt, shorts, and sneakers, so it didn't matter if he got wet. He headed down the coast road, his huge legs pumping into the wind, his eyes squinted against the dust. When he reached the other town, it was windy, but clear and warm, tourists heading for the beaches. He could see the tremendous clouds over the mountain and what looked like a dense curtain of rain heading towards the apartment. The whole storm system seemed to be generated directly out of the mountain itself. He thought of her alone in the apartment with the storm approaching. She would be worrying about him, not realizing he was clear out of it, sitting against a tree and having a cup of coffee. He looked at the apartment in his mind, room by room and thought what ought to be done. They had had strong winds before, so she knew to latch the shutters and not leave a door or window open in such a way that the wind could slam it shut and shatter the glass. But they had not up to now had rain. He remembered a stupid design flaw. The flat roof of the apartment complex drained down a large pipe which idiotically emptied onto their black-walled balcony and thence out a small hole in the floor of the balcony. In a real torrential downpour, he estimated, that hole might be just fast enough to empty the balcony and keep it from backing up and flooding the kitchen. But, and here was a problem, there was a complicated grate fitted into the hole, which he should have removed as soon as he saw it, but had not. It created enough of an obstruction that it would stop the balcony from draining fast enough. He had not bothered to tell her to remove it in case of a storm, imagining that he would be there himself to do it. He thought of her coping with the flood, putting up towels against the door to dam the flood, bailing into the sink, and then he saw clearly the refrigerator with its electric motor on the bottom. Two inches of water in the kitchen—which she would be standing in—would reach the motor and short it out, electrocuting her.

Now he rode the bike with the wind and like the wind, his half-full thermos lying beside the road where he dropped it. Ahead of him the clouds thickened. Then he was over wet ground and deep puddles where the storm had passed, plowing through six inches of flood water in low parts of the road. The black wall of rain beyond which all was obscured was still ahead of him. Then he heard and felt the first big splats of water and in moments the rain was so thick he could barely see. To make things worse, as he crossed the edge of the cyclone, the wind shifted around until it was driving straight against him again, blinding him and now stinging him with hail, like shrapnel from the lightning bursting all around him. His broad body worked like a negative sail, an air anchor, holding him back as in a dream of running underwater. His massive thighs were nonetheless equal to any temporal wind and he pumped grimly, and, if such a word could be appropriate here, remorselessly. Then he had reached the edge of town, the rain coming with new fury, and turned up the side street off the front, leapt off the bike, feeling with surprise the sudden weakness in his legs, sprinted up the flight of stairs, threw open the front door and punched the off button on the circuit breaker box. She was in the kitchen, towels against the door, bailing frantically into the sink. The water had just reached two inches deep. He pushed past her onto the back balcony, reached down into the deep swirling water for the grate, pulled it out and threw it as far as he could. The sky was already clearing.

Time was passing, and if in her patient and dreamy way she might someday get around to painting the mountain, she still had already missed thousands of changes never again to be repeated. He couldn't stand it anymore, and rented a car and drove across the island to the one city and bought an expensive camera and a heavy surveyor's tripod. He was too busy to spend years studying art and training his hand to reproduce what his eyes saw. So why not get a machine, a piece of apparatus, that will do it at once, and more accurately than the hand could ever do? He felt in his pride of the machine the faintest contempt for the patient art of his wife. That was a bit mean, so he altered that to feel instead guilty that he was trespassing on her turf, or sorry that he would so easily and quickly accomplish what she was still only contemplating. The dreamers and the doers. Of course it was her idea. He wouldn't have thought of it. But that's always the way, the reason we need the dreamers on this planet.

Yet it was not guilt or sympathy he felt setting his camera up on its tripod and aiming it at the mountain. It was self-consciousness, because though she said nothing, and seemed outwardly to show only the most generous interest, he felt she would be judging him, judging his results by criteria he was not altogether sure of. He looked through the viewfinder, aware that he was repeating the process of holding the paper with the hole cut out at arm's distance in front of him. His was only a more sophisticated version. And though when she was doing it, it was all he could do to restrain himself from taking it out of her hands and looking himself and telling her just where to do it from, it seemed so obvious to him, here now that he was actually doing it from this spot rather than that, he felt the whole weight of her competency bearing down on him. He actually felt himself sweating with this new kind of labor. He began to understand her exasperation with him at times, and wanted to turn and say Let me do this my way!—when he noticed she was in the bathroom running a bath and singing to herself.

One angle of the mountain did seem to show it the way he most often thought of it, and he locked the tripod into place. He realized he had already learned something. What he wanted was not *the* mountain, but rather, the mountain as *he* thought of it. At any rate he thought that *the* mountain, and the mountain the way *he* thought of it, were pretty close. He took the light reading carefully—it was altering as he took it, clouds crossing, then leaving the sun—and pressed the cable release to take his first picture. Click. He had caught it. This time it hadn't got away.

Throughout the day, as he did other things, he watched the mountain out of the corner of his eye, and as it altered, he snapped it. She was at the table painting a tiny white autumn flower. The last picture on the roll was a several-second-long exposure of the sunset, which this evening was like a gorgeous swirling bruise. He felt it would definitely be the most spectacular. He had made a few notes with each exposure, describing the state of the mountain in a few concise words. He had a feeling after all that if he approached it systematically he would find that the seemingly endless changes would reduce themselves to a manageable few that repeated themselves. Perhaps a relatively small number of pictures, say a hundred, would tell the whole story of the mountain. In the morning he took the film to a shop that promised 24 hour service.

In the end it was three full days before he got them back. He had been in the shop a dozen times, his temper beginning to fray. But he smiled openly like a child when the shopkeeper, equally relieved, held up the packet as he entered. One satisfaction was that in all this time his wife had only managed to paint two petals on her flower. He ripped open the package as he was leaving the shop and could hardly believe what he saw. The giant mountain that had dominated his imagination for nearly two months came out in his pictures like a tiny pimple. Not only that, the colors were all wrong, much too blue at times, much too red at others, and everything he had seen as sharp and crisp was pale and washed out. The sunset was particularly flat and uninteresting. There was going to be more to this than he thought, and he set his jaw grimly, and went back into the shop and bought a big book on photography.

He read it straight through, and returned to the pertinent pages several times. He rented the car again and went back to the city and this time bought some filters to cut out haze and to correct color, and a longer focal length lens to bring the mountain forward to give it the magnitude he saw with his eye.

In the meantime she had completed her small perfect painting. The flower itself was blown and dry and unrecognizable, having faded in two days.

If things won't give in to your first rush, then you must be persistent and systematic. With an uneasy feeling that he was backing off slightly from his first resolve to record Big Dog in all its moods, he decided, for an initial objective, he would record it perfectly in *one* of its moods. He was so eager to begin he was up before dawn setting up the tripod. The sun, rising behind his back, illuminated the mountain before anything else, in a delicate faded pink, almost white, and it seemed like a fragile cone of infolded petals, until the sun was fully disengaged from the earth, when it took on the harsh black shadows and the glaring rocky face of its true substance. That's what he was waiting for, and he photographed it with his long lens to bring it up tall in the sky, crowding over the tops of the closer mountains, and he tried it with each filter, with every combination of aperture and duration, carefully noting down in his notebook which combinations he had used. It took the pictures a week this time to come back from the 24-hour place, but they were terrific. There was the overbearing face, the metallic sky, the strong relief shadows. He showed them to her, and she said, "Yes, that's it, that's really good," and the child-like smile was on his face.

She had found a tiny winter flower in bloom, and brought a blossom and a bit of leaf back, and set it in a jar to paint. But the old couple across the way needed her. She had been doing their shopping for them—the old man's pension check was so meager, and food was so expensive, she had been secretly augmenting it when she bought their food—and doing a few other chores. She had started out with gestures, but had word by word picked up the local dialect from them until now they conversed quite well. But the man was ill, growing worse. His wife needed all her time to care for him, so she had been doing everything else, cooking, washing. After she and the wife got the old man through a particularly bad spell, she found her winter flower had dried out past the point of her being able to recreate it in paints.

For a few days he was complacent, but then he went back and looked at his pictures more critically. With the blush of newness off them, they seemed less good, compared less favorably with the actual mountain. Further, he could see now how sloppily they had been developed, stains, dust spots, small patches where the color was the wrong tone. He rented the car, and went back to the city and this time returned with an enlarger and darkroom equipment. He took more pictures, then blacked out the bathroom and went in and developed his first roll. He liked the instant service. The waiting had killed him. And he was absolutely careful about dust, and keeping the temperature right, and of course had made sure all his chemicals were fresh. He started with a roll of black and white, figuring after he got the hang of it, he would return to color. But when he showed her the results she said, "Do you know what? It's better in black and white than it was in color." "How can that be?" he said, but he was only arguing from logic, because now that she had said it, he could see it too.

He caught the mountain in a few more moods, and was at least moderately pleased with the results. He thought he was learning better to make the camera record what he saw. But there were calls on his time as well. He was becoming quite proficient with the language, and was now helping the budding language school—it had been started by talented and ambitious young students with not much money or expertise. Rather than using textbooks based on some professor's notion of the most used words and grammatical constructions, they had adopted his technique of taping actual speech in the shops and on the streets, and using that—the language really used every day—as the basis of each lesson. The school, as the tourists began returning in the spring, began operating profitably and gained a reputation, and they got a publisher interested in the textbook they were putting together based on their new method. He showed them how to set up records and keep books, drafted the English parts of the textbook, and even went with them to take their petition to the provincial government to be licensed as a corporation, so that very often the camera sat pointing at the mountain through its various moods, but no one was there to press the cable release. And when he did complete a roll of film, it sat for weeks before he had a chance to develop it.

He had not lost any of his 60 extra pounds, but nevertheless bought some running shoes and started running. "I don't know why you bother to get advice from people if you're not going to follow it," she said. "I probably know my strengths and weaknesses better than a doctor who has only seen me a couple of times," he said. "You don't have any sense at all of your weaknesses. That's why you worked too hard and had to see the doctor in the first place." "It was just nerves, nothing physical." "He said that your heart—" "My heart's okay." "Your problem is you don't respect anyone or anything except yourself. You'd think after you got that head injury in college you would have realized you're not immortal." "You'll notice it's my head I've gone on to make my living with. Your problem is you respect everything and everybody *except* yourself. You have no concept of how strong you are in your own way. And how good. You're like an angel come back to earth sometimes. People think *I'm* good, just because I'm connected to you."

There was certainly no way she could respond to that, and he took off downstairs running.

Spring was progressing, the weather clearing. The mountain, which had often been obscured behind clouds and mist, was now visible again, but the camera and tripod, in the way of everything she wanted to do in the front room, was seldom used, though he often paused meditatively to look through the view finder. They were still trying to get the school officially licensed but the red tape was incredible. She noticed he was beginning to eat more, a bad sign. He kept up with his running faithfully, each day running as far up the mountain as the road went and back. Most days now this sweaty shaggy bear of a man, looking even more ludicrous, brought back in his big hand a tiny new spring flower for her to paint. She was deluged by the bounty. Twenty flowers withered and died while she struggled to paint one. It might take her all day to paint one petal—and that was when she had all day to work on it. The old man was better, but the wife was ill, and this was worse than the other way around, because she had to nurse his wife as well as shop and clean, plus trying to keep the old man from sinking into depression. Then the woman was well, and both of them had come through another winter, the time when old people die if they are going to, and they were fiercely proud to have survived again. She had part of the day to herself again, and sat down to her paints and a tiny flower. He had taken a day off too, and set off running right after breakfast. She finished doing the breakfast dishes and came out to look at the mountain. The morning had started clear and warm without a leaf moving. But as she looked she saw a huge thunderhead rising up directly out of the summit of the mountain. She looked with her binoculars and saw it seething and pumping. There was not a sound. She tried to go to her painting, but in a few minutes was back looking at the mountain. The cloud rose ten thousand feet straight above it in the still air, solid as an iceberg. While she looked she saw a flicker of light through it. Trees only grew to above the 3000 foot line, so for the last few miles he would be above them, and would himself be the highest point on the exposed road. She wrung her hands helplessly. Two thick bolts of lightning struck the mountain in quick succession, jarring into it like fists. She set her jaw grimly, and went down to the garage two blocks from them, the one he always went to, and rented a car. "I know I'm just being stupid," she said to herself, but she drove like the wind. She came out above the trees and saw the lone runner near the end of the road several switchbacks ahead of her. The sky was black but there was complete stillness in the air. She downshifted and spun around the switchbacks, sending up a skein of gravel against the safety railings. From 100 yards distance she could see the hair was standing straight up around his head like an eerie aurora. He ran on, totally absorbed in what he was doing.

He reached the top of the road, the turn-around point, shrugging the stopwatch out of his pocket and raising it up to look at his elapsed time. With the other hand he was trying abstractedly to smooth down his hair. *Heart attack, good-bye...*

She didn't hear the stupendous crack of thunder either, she was too intent on getting the car stopped and getting out beside him, which she did in seconds, smoke still rising from the charred pieces remaining of his sneakers, a black after-image dividing her vision. She rolled him onto his back and put the side of her head to his vast sinewed rib cage. He was not breathing, nor could she detect a heartbeat. This was one process she did know something about. Because of the time she spent with old people, she had made herself take an advanced first aid course. She thumped at the huge chest, the defunct bellows, with her tiny fists, but knew that was not enough, and stood up on his chest and bounced her whole weight on it at one second intervals, and the heart, like a well-tuned engine, caught at the first try. Then she jutted out the sandpapery lower jaw, to open the wind pipe, and covered his mouth with hers, and blow in her child's breath as hard as she could, and again he took the spark of life from her, and was breathing. She has no idea how she got him into the car, only knows that the next day all the muscles down her side were pulled and were never quite right again.

In the hospital they told her she had plainly saved his life by being there at that second and knowing just what to do. It was a miracle, they kept saying. She began to find that a bit insulting. They found he had lost 60 pounds at the moment he was struck, body fluids simply vaporized, and every muscle in his body was shredded, and his calves and feet severely burned. He was already fully conscious and discussing with the doctor what steps he would need to take in his recovery, and how soon he could think about starting up his running again. He looked up at her, grinning. "You've got your nerve, following me around and thinking you know better than I do."

Everyone, except him, was amazed at the speed of his recovery. In less time than can be imagined he was back at the apartment, getting around a little bit on crutches. She gave him all her time, but he was very undemanding, a surprisingly good, obedient patient. Also he was obsessed again. This time, of all things, with photographing a plain drinking glass not quite full of water. Oh, he continued to photograph the whole mountain, and he continued, by telephone, doing some of the business of the language school, but maybe he had been just a bit chastened, and wanted to cover his bets by also trying to come at the whole by looking closely at one of its parts.

"You can't believe how challenging this is," he told her. "I must have taken fifty pictures of this thing and I still am just learning what to see in it."

She for her part continued her exacting painting of the single leaf, the single flower, but at moments during the day she let her point of focus come out a bit. She picked up her sheet of plotted-out outlines of the mountain. None of the paintings took her more than two or three minutes to do. She filled sheet after sheet, her confidence and speed growing. She had been to that mountain, and felt she knew something about it. He had arrived at one position, one angle of light, that he thought was perfect, and he thought he was beginning to learn exactly how he wanted to develop the negative. By then however their time was up and they left the island.

Norman Lavers earned his Ph.D. at the University of Iowa. He has taught at the university level in the U.S.A. and Thailand, and has lived in various parts of Europe, Asia and North America. His published works include volumes of literary criticism, a novel and a collection of short stories. He has received Iowa Writers Workshop and National Endowment for the Arts fellowships, the O. Henry award and the Hohenberg prize for fiction.

"The children aren't guilty, are they?"

Home

BY ALES RYBAK

ALL that day and night, before she and Lesik were arrested, Olga lived with the premonition of disaster.

Yesterday, at deepest midnight, as the wind raved outside the walls of the house, hurling great handfuls of dry snow against the window panes, and the wolves howled somewhere close by in the forest, Ivan came to the farm together with three partisans.

Olga had not seen her husband for over a month and, overjoyed, rushed out into the hall to fetch what she had from the barrel to feed the men. But Ivan told her they were in a hurry with some urgent business and, if everything went well, he would be back in a day or two.

The partisans ate a little frozen lard with onion and potato—there was no bread—then lit cigarettes and began to get themselves ready. Ivan pulled off his sodden boots. They were falling apart; the sole on the right one was fastened on by string. He put on his old, patched, but warm felt boots and went through to the side-room where Lesik was sleeping in a cradle by the stove. He gave his son a light kiss and gazed admiringly at him a while, before embracing and kissing Olga lovingly, as she stood there strained and silent.

Olga wanted to accompany them, but Ivan would not let her come farther than the yard. The snow had drifted above the fence and piled up almost knee-high along the path to the narrow gate behind the cowshed, even though the path had been swept that evening.

The snowstorm gave no sign of abating. Olga stood at the gate and stared out sadly into the thick, murky, gray gloom that had swallowed up Ivan.

After lunch, Adolya ran over from the neighboring farmstead and told her furtively, almost in a whisper, as if someone might hear them, that in the night a German train carrying tanks and guns had been blown up on the railway...From early morning, a large number of Germans and their local henchmen, *polizeis*, had driven into the neighboring village of Chubovka. No one knew what they were after or what they had decided to do, but everyone was alarmed.

Adolya lamented and sighed a little, then trotted straight back to her house, oddly churning up the snow with her feet as she went. Olga stood at the window, pale, her lips bitten till they bled. The news of the blown-up train was encouraging but she knew full well who had been responsible for it that night. She was worried sick by what Adolya had told her about the Germans in Chubovka. They would not be poking their noses in there for nothing.

Olga did not get a moment's sleep that night. She stood for hours in the kitchen by the window that looked out towards Chubovka, listening attentively. At one point she suddenly thought she heard the sound of a car close by and rushed in to the side-room, where Lesik was sweetly snuffing, barring the cradle and ready to lay her hands on anyone who came near the child.

Only towards morning, sapped of strength, did she lie down fully clothed on the bed and fall asleep immediately. She was woken by Lesik, who was hungry. Olga fed and changed him, and went to the shed for firewood.

Occupied as she was with her work, she did not hear the two Germans and a polizei come into the house, but a moment later, Lesik's loud cry brought her rushing back into the side-room. The polizei—Olga knew him by sight—hesitated to follow her in, but stood at the door and ordered her, in a loud voice so that the Germans would hear, to dress herself and the child.

"I'm not going anywhere with a little baby!" Olga cried in despair. "What am I supposed to do in Chubovka?"

"You'll go nice and quietly," the polizei hissed between her teeth. "You've sat long enough in your hornets' nest."

Olga could only vaguely remember the rest, as she, Lesik and the others were driven into the barn. Everything was obscured by thoughts of Ivan. Where was he? What had happened to him? She saw the road to Chubovka in a blur, as if an eternity had passed since then, the deep, above the knees, snow, the policeman shoving her for dragging along so deathly slow, her falling to one side with Lesik and collapsing in a drift as the soldiers jeered. Fortunately, it was soft, and Lesik did not feel the fall, nor start to cry. But Olga got snow in her sleeves and felt boots.

Only in the barn, which stuck out miserably to the side of the road about 200 meters outside Chubovka, as they shoved the women and children and feeble old men in, did Olga realize with terror, from odd snatches of conversation, that these were all families of partisans.

The barn roof let through light like a sieve, and a fine snow fell from the low, gray sky through the lathing, where a few wisps of dark straw clung here and there. The walls had also sunk and leaned to one side. A persistent, stubborn wind blew through the cracks, where there had once been moss, chilling to the bone. No one had strength left to resist the cold. The women begged heaven rather send them deliverance through death, than bear such torments. Huddled in one corner, by a pile of mice-riddled, old hay, they tried somehow to shield their children from the wind, stripping off everything warm they wore and wrapping them up in it.

But they were soon all driven out beyond the village, where the German garrison was located. They were barely able to move their legs, so weakened and numbed with cold were they. True, it was somewhat easier walking along the road, but there was still so much snow. Ahead of them the Germans drove a vehicle, leaving deep ruts behind. The polizeis—there were plenty of them too—walked on foot at the back, shoving those who lagged behind with their rifle-butts, and shouting.

Passing a field, the road first led through a young pine forest, which soon gave way to tall, straight pines. The wind was less sharp here; it did not pierce so. It became warmer. While Olga's feet felt more alive as she walked, her hands were almost completely numb. At this moment, however, she thought least of herself and where they were being driven. Pressing Lesik closer to herself, she tried somehow to push back the blanket to get a glimpse at his little face. Her wooden fingers would not obey her and, with blue lips, she silently begged her son to bear out just a little longer. She had no idea what she was hoping for. It was as if she were in a heavy, agonizing dream, an incomprehensible oblivion.

Only when an explosion roared some hundred meters in front, did she stir and raise her head. An unseen, mighty force threw the oak planks of the bridge high in the air and the heavy vehicle with the German soldiers overturned into the deep ditch.

Almost simultaneously with the explosion, from behind the bushes to the left of the highway, someone shouted with all his might. "Women get down!" Olga at last realized what was happening and quickly slid down the snow of the steep slope, holding Lesik in her arms. At almost the same moment the air was rent by machine-gun fire.

At first there was the joy of seeing Ivan again. In the heart of the forest, when the terrible fear had receded, they kissed each other without embarrassment in full view of the others and wept, without hiding their tears. Ivan sat her in the sleigh and wrapped her in a sheepskin. He took Lesik in one arm and stroked her cheek with his other hand. In all the excitement and turmoil, her fear for the child subsided. It seemed the worst had passed her and the boy; any moment now they would reach a safe, warm place and mother and father would not let their little one come to harm.

Olga did not remember her wild cries on realizing Lesik was dead, once they were back in the partisan dug-out in the camp after a four-hour ride across the forest. Only a month later did Ivan tell her about her heartrending wail.

At first, when they buried Lesik, it seemed she might pull through, though the grief stunned and dazed her. She chose a place for the grave not far from the camp. It was a small, round glade, where the young birches grew thick, stretching upwards, and in the center towered two ancient, giant oaks. A thick white layer of snow lay all around, but one sensed how quiet and green it would be there in the spring.

They did not lay Lesik in a coffin, but in a wooden trough, hammered over on top with plywood. Ivan was alarmed by her dull, indifferent expression and the way she did not shed a single tear. They might as well have been burying some unknown child and not her own.

Afterwards, she took to her bed. She stared obstinately into the distance with glassy eyes, would neither eat nor speak and barely recognized anyone. The doctor's assistant in the detachment, an old bearded man, gestured helplessly and could suggest nothing. Olga lost weight, her face grew yellow. Ivan sat by her side day and night, relieved of duties by the detachment commander out of compassion for Olga.

The same time a year later, both familiar and unfamiliar paths led Olga back home. She was saddened by her parting with Ivan. On their last evening together, he had talked of how they would live, once they had completely beaten the enemy scum. Even though they had flung the enemy far back the Nazis were still baring their teeth, murdering, burning and plundering. He could not leave the detachment. He did not have the right to do so. But Olga should go home, to their village liberated and cleansed of the fascist filth, and look after the house—if it was still in one piece—perhaps plant or sow something by the time he came back. After all, life must go on. She had done enough fighting and seen enough horror. The whole year they had been risking their lives together, been out on assignments together and sat out together in the marsh, pursued by police hounds. They had been through everything, but they had survived, thank God.

Nonetheless, Ivan warned her not to leave the beaten track, nor spend the night in the first place she came to, for anything might happen. She might run up against some Fritz or a polizei, or one of the packs of hungry wolves that had multiplied into thousands during the war.

Towards evening she was nearing the farm. It was already dark and the thick, warm air had changed to a light, night frost, as often happens in these parts at the end of March. During the day, the firs and pines along the way had swollen with the damp and stood silent and thoughtful. Their silence even frightened her a little.

All that was left of the barn, where she and Lesik had been thrown by the Nazis that time, were its charred remains. Passing on a little further, Olga almost fainted. Her legs aching from the hard, almost three-day walk, buckled, and only with great effort did she force herself to stay upright and not fall onto the road.

Although it was already dark, a terrible picture opened before her eyes: there was nothing left of Chubovka. Only skeletal chimney stocks of some half-demolished stoves stood out darkly. Somewhere a lonely tomcat began to howl. And the people, what had the fascists done to the people? Surely they could not all be dead?

Olga gasped for breath; she felt as if any moment she would choke. Almost losing consciousness she bent down, gathered up a handful of snow and placed it against her face, then thrust her wet, frozen hand inside, close to her heart. It relieved her slightly, but she could walk no further. She took the pack from her shoulders. She and Ivan had shoved all they possessed into it: half a loaf of bread, a few boiled potatoes in their skins, two pieces of soap, a little salt and a box of matches. She sat down on top of it. Though it did not weigh much, it had rubbed and pulled on her shoulders on the journey.

Where should she go now? If they had completely destroyed Chubovka with its school, shop and village soviet where she and Ivan had registered their marriage then there would probably be no trace of their small village left.

Olga stood up heavily, then somehow pulled herself together and threw the pack over her shoulder. She did not like to walk through Chubovka—through what was left of it—and turned off decisively to one side, setting off across the snow. It had settled, but was still deep.

It was already quite dark, but Olga walked straight ahead across the fields, unafraid of losing her way. She could have found her house with her eyes closed. She recognized from a distance every little hill and hollow, every boulder and bush, though they had lost their clear contours in the mist.

Suddenly she smelt smoke. Her heart missed a beat with aching hope. Was it possible misfortune had passed them by and she would cross the threshold of her own home?

There was the Tomash's farmstead, its buildings standing out darkly. Even in the darkness she could see a whitish smoke twisting about in the chimney. Adolya was probably preparing for her one-legged Tomash his usual dumplings for supper. And there was her own house! But what was this? Why was a feeble, barely visible light filtering through the darkness of the night from the kitchen? Who could have moved in to their house?

She thought it better to call in on Adolya first. Adolya would tell her what had happened in Chubovka. She would also tell her who had moved into her house. That was the main thing, of course.

Adolya was bustling about in the kitchen by a chipped tub. She was bent over it, washing some tiny potatoes, the size of nuts, and putting them in an iron pot, and did not even look up at Olga as she came in through the door. Olga was just going to greet her, when Adolya barked out, her head down, "Where the devil have you been the whole evening? You've not brought any firewood in for tomorrow, not even a single log. I'm the only one doing anything here..."

Olga coughed and Adolya stood up sharply. "Olga! You're alive!" she cried. "I thought it was my dawdler...He set off to Gorash's before dark to fetch some matches and he's still not back. What can he be doing so long?" She embraced Olga, distractedly happy, and pressed her face wet with tears to Olga's cheek. "I never thought I'd see you again...Well, I knew the partisans had rescued you that time at the bridge, but so much time has passed since then."

They both sat down on the bench and began to cry. Olga told

Adolya about herself and Lesik, and how she had been afterwards. Adolya wiped her eyes with her apron.

"What happened...at Chubovka...? Did they kill everyone...?" Olga asked at last.

Adolya froze, her face whitened and her hands began to tremble on her knees.

"Go on, tell me!" Olga shouted. She did not recognize her own voice.

"You probably saw as you went past...It wasn't that long ago...About two months...They rushed in all in black...like a flock of crows...Wanted to find out who'd finished off the village elder...But who could have seen it? A cur's death for a cur..." Adolya fell silent. "They rounded up the whole of Chubovka into the barn and set it on fire. Burnt them alive, young and old. They took their revenge on them for helping the partisans, and for hating the new authorities installed by the Germans and for the fact that practically all the men and lads were either in the army or had run off to the partisans into the forest."

Olga sat there petrified. Her unseeing eyes were filled with such grief, that Adolya took fright. She stood up and clasped her hands together.

"Look at me, I've not even welcomed you properly or asked you to take your coat off. Take your coat off, dear. It's warm here, thank God. Perhaps Tomash'll turn up soon and we can spend the evening together! The dumplings in the oven are almost ready!"

"I must go." Olga roused herself. Adolya realized from her neighbor's tone that she wanted to know who was over there in her house.

As if trying to justify herself, Adolya began to sob.

"There's a polizei's wife there...with a child. Not local people, they were on the run with the Germans, escaping. When they came I told them you'd be coming back. The polizei almost killed me when I said that. He kept running about, waving his revolver and making threats. But he was scared stiff himself, what with our lads putting on the pressure and not giving those skunks a moment's peace! On top of that he'd got his wife pregnant and due soon. Then she fell ill, so he left her here alone with child and took off."

Olga shook violently.

"In my house? A polizei's wife?"

She could not remember how she seized her pack and hurried away from Adolya. She did not feel any tiredness or pain in her legs, but strode over to her yard with heavy, deliberate steps, sinking in places up to the knee in the snow. She was animated by one thought and desire: to get inside her house and chuck out all this uninvited lodger's belongings, fling everything out on the street, so there was nothing left of her. Clear off where she came from! Let her try to catch her polizei up; she might make it yet! Thought she'd chosen herself a nice little corner, did she? Wanted everything ready on a plate? Well, they'd lorded it over us long enough.

The door was bolted and Olga began to knock furiously, putting in to her blows some unknown reserve of strength. A minute later she heard the familiar creak of floorboards from the kitchen and a feeble, woman's voice asked worriedly, "Who's there?"

"Open the door!" Olga kicked the door impatiently this time. Even the window pane rattled loudly.

There was a short, anxious silence inside, then a busy stamping and shuffling of feet, and the same distracted voice sighed, "Just a moment. Oh, what is it?"

Behind the door, she could hear someone searching for the bolt in the dark. Can't find it, Olga thought wickedly, but you managed all right getting into someone else's house, didn't you?

At last the bolt screeched metallically. Olga waited, then shoved the door open and, leaving it flung wide, stepped into the kitchen at almost the same moment as the other woman. Her eye was caught immediately by the dimmed lamp on the table, its wick turned down. In its feeble light, she made out a small, young woman with a pale, blood-drained face and frozen expression. She was leaning against the wall, her arms stretching out wide in front of her, as if defending herself from someone, a large belly visible behind them...Beside her, clutching at her skirt, a boy of five or six with light brown hair stood barefoot on the uncovered floor, sobbing quietly.

Olga laid her pack down silently on the stool, hung up her

sheepskin coat on a nail by the door and glanced round the room, as if checking everything was in the same place it had been in the house a year ago. She could not make out anything in the dark. Feeling a draught from the yard, she went and closed the door. She had to say something, fling some words in this unknown woman's face that would cut to the quick. But strangely, those cruel, just words inexplicably froze on her lips. She looked at the motionless young woman and the boy once again. The woman's face was still white, but now grimaced with pain, and Olga sensed some tightly tuned string had suddenly been snapped. "Well, what are we going to do?" Olga hissed, frowning, more for appearance's sake than anything else. She didn't want to get soft or to keep silent.

"Just a moment and we'll be off somewhere," the young woman mumbled quickly and began to rush about the room.

She grabbed her own and the boy's clothes, as well as some other things that came to hand, and flung them in a pile in the middle of the kitchen. She pulled out a motley, homemade counterpane from somewhere and bent down to tie it all up into a bundle, but then groaned strangely and sank onto the floor.

Olga took fright. It was obvious from the way the young woman bit her lips till they bled, gasped for breath and writhed, clutching the lower part of her belly, that she was in pain and might go into labor at any moment, if she had not already started. One could not just stand there with idle hands. After all, she was a human being, a woman. Perhaps she had never felt so sick in her life. She needed help. On top of that, the boy began to scream, throwing himself at his mother. "Mummy...get up! Get up, Mummy!" he cried, wiping the tears over his face with his fist.

Olga took his hand, stroked his soft light brown hair and felt a lump rise in her throat. What on earth was going on?

She sat the boy down on a bench in the corner, told him not to move or cry, turned up the flame in the lamp and bent down over the young woman. She was obviously getting steadily worse. Olga put a jacket under the woman's head—she did not know whose it was—and decided to run straight over to Adolya. Perhaps together they might help alleviate the woman's suffering, particularly since

Olga knew Adolya was not a novice at this sort of thing.

Fortunately, Adolya had not yet gone to bed; she and Tomash were in the middle of supper. "What's going on over at your place?" she asked worriedly, seeing her neighbor on the doorstep without either a sheepskin coat or scarf.

"The...lodger—she's feeling bad."

"She's early," Adolya guessed, and taking a pot of hot water out of the stove—luckily it had been on since morning—she poured some into a large, earthenware jug and pulled a clean towel out of the chest. She quickly got dressed and went out with Olga.

By midnight, exhausted, they realized they could do nothing to save the young woman. She was still bleeding from the birth. Adolya had to run home twice more to warm up some water and boil some herbs on the coals in the stove, because Olga's house was not heated.

Picking up the child—a boy, and obviously premature—Olga helped Adolya as best she could.

When she found a free moment, she popped out to the shed and hunted round for firewood in the dark, but could not find a single log and came back empty-handed into the cold house. The elder boy was still crying and would not stop, and however much Olga tried to persuade him, he would not go to sleep in the bed they had made up for him.

The young woman was bleeding heavily. She was delirious and kept trying to run off somewhere. She came round towards morning, as Adolya, feeling exhausted, trudged home for some kerosene for the empty lamp, scraping the door behind her. With her deep-set eyes, glistening with tears, the woman beckoned Olga to bend closer to her and asked in a quiet and guilty voice, to be shown the child. Seeing it was a boy, both alive and well, she suddenly began to sob and beat her head against the floor. "The children aren't guilty, are they? The children won't be punished?" she found strength to ask, moving her dry, chapped lips with difficulty, as she began to lose consciousness once more.

Olga got up off the bed, fumbled about in the dark for the matches on top of the cupboard, and striking one, looked up at the clock ticking loudly on the wall. It was not yet four o'clock. She went over to the cradle and listened attentively. The child was asleep, breathing feebly.

Even the previous evening she had not thought he would survive, that he would live only hours, not even days. His tiny body was blue, and his little face the size of a fist, which had been as wrinkled as a baked apple, was now even smaller. The child did not seem to show any sign of life. Something stirred within Olga, a thread snapped inside. An age-old, feminine instinct seemed to protest: what are you doing? Here is a helpless, defenseless child before you. Who else if not you will take on the care for this new life?

She chewed up some soft bread and wound it in a piece of clean gauze. Then she dipped it in some sugared water and carefully inserted the handmade dummy into the child's mouth. But he would not suck. Olga was worried to distraction and sat there for a few moments before deciding to call over on Adolya again. Perhaps she might be able to suggest something.

Adolya did not know what to do either. It had been easy before the war: you simply went to the hospital in Chubovka. Now there was nothing left of the hospital or Chubovka.

After some thought, Adolya suggested giving the child a good wash, then a steam, in warm water, while she boiled up some herbs and tried to get the baby to drink the infusion from a spoon.

By evening, Olga had heated the stove up properly, prepared a clean sheet and warmed the blanket. Adolya was weaving spells over the herbs.

When they had done everything as planned, and Adolya had gone home, Olga was overjoyed to see the child had indeed got some color back. He moved his little lips once or twice in his sleep and seemed to be asking for food. Olga put the sugared bread in the gauze back in his mouth and went out into the kitchen to dilute some milk with boiled water.

Again the child would not suck the bread, but by daybreak he had drunk almost half a glass of milk. Probably the herbs had helped! She fed him from a spoon, because she did not have a feeding bottle.

She did not go back to bed, but went out into the yard.

Low, heavy storm-clouds densely covered the sky and drizzle alternated with snow. Only in the east, beyond Gorash's farm, was a narrow, finger-thin, bright strip drawn across the dark leaden sky, as if someone had stuck a scrap of clean paper up there. This scrap gave some hope that, perhaps, the sun might peep through and spring set in at last. She had no more strength left to wait for the good weather.

Olga attached particular hope to the spring and warm weather. Above all, that of seeing Ivan again, of course.

How she missed him now at home! How she missed his caresses, his calm good sense. The house badly needed a man's touch; the farm had fallen into complete disrepair and she did not know where to begin, what to do first.

Olga stood a while outside, then went back into the house. She did not light the wick lamp, but fumbled in the corner for the rusty axe with its jagged blade, chopped the wood and began to light the stove. She must cook something, make herself something to eat. She could barely move her legs. Tomash had taken the elder boy away to the district center the day before and got him into a children's home.

Olga tried to shake off her heavy thoughts and vague forebodings, but nothing seemed to help. She wandered around all day in a dream, but later decided to go to Gorash's to ask for some milk for the child.

It was dusk. The sun had already set, and on that side above the forest, the sky was unusually red, like blood. Surely another village was not burning? Who could've set it on fire now? There would have been smoke too. However much she stared—the circles began to swim before her eyes—she could not make out anything that would have indicated a fire.

On Olga's way back, the road had dried a little and it was easier to walk, her feet did not slip so. She skirted a slope, beyond which the soft, dark snow still lay weeping in a glade hidden from the sun, and climbed a small hill. From here she looked out over the familiar, now darkened road and froze. A skinny horse harnessed to a trap stood by the fencing next to her gate. Even from a distance she could make out its ribs beneath the dark-chestnut coat. Who can it be? She set off at a run towards the yard. Surely it can't be?

An officer with an exhausted face came stooping out of the house and Olga's legs numbed and buckled. The officer was wearing a new overcoat and a star shone on his shoulder straps. A major, she noted silently in passing, with an empty sleeve tucked in his belt. Where's he from, the front? But the horse and trap...

"I'm from the military registration and enlistment office," the major said, when she had come closer. "Is your name Lagatskaya?"

"Yes. What's it about?" Once again Olga felt her heart thumping painfully in her breast and a sense of foreboding gripped and chilled her.

A moment later, back inside the house, she stared with deadened, empty but dry eyes at the piece of paper, which the major had taken out of his map-case and held out to her.

"I'm sorry for bringing you the sad news," she heard faintly. "If you need anything, get in touch with us at the office."

The major went outside, trying not to stamp his boots. She stood there motionless, watching through the window pane as he untied the horse, straightened something in the trap, then got in and pulled the reins up sharp.

A month later, when Olga had recovered a little and all around her spring had begun in earnest, she made up her mind to go to Sadki. She carried the baby in her arms, wrapped in a flannelette blanket. She just called him "baby" because she still had not thought of any name.

The rural soviet occupied half of someone's house and was fortunately open.

The youngish chairman was wearing a military shirt and riding breeches. He sat Olga down in an armchair by the table, rummaged about at first in his papers, then pushed them to one side and asked, "What can I do for you?"

"Well," Olga looked up at him, "I have to register this boy, my son...There wasn't any time..."

"Of course." The chairman cheered up. "That's quite simple. I thought you were going to ask for something. People come here every day, but what on earth can I do for them? We've got nothing—no seed, no flour, no nails—nothing." He leaned back wearily in his chair and put his hands on the table. Only then did Olga see he had no fingers on his right hand, only stumps. How does he manage to write? she thought horrified. However, the chairman picked up the wooden pen holder with an easy, deft movement and dipped the pen into the ink-pot.

"What's the surname?" he asked in his hoarse voice.

"Lagatskaya."

"No, I mean what's the boy's surname? Lagatsky? Right, so let's get that down—Lagatsky. First name?"

"I don't know yet. I've not thought about it. Perhaps...?"

"You shouldn't think too hard about it. Let me see...I rather like Dmitri, Dima, for short. A good name. Well?"

"Yes," Olga agreed. "Let's call him Dima, Dmitri. It suits him."

"Right, what patronymic?"

"Ivanovich," Olga answered quickly, so that the chairman would have no doubts.

Coming out onto the street, she sighed with relief, as if she had shaken an enormous weight off her shoulders, and pressed her son close to her breast. He was her son now.

Some time later, with the help of the military registration and enlistment office and of the very same major, Olga left her village. After a tearful parting with Adolya and Tomash, she moved to another, distant village, where she knew no one and no one knew her.

The Byelorussian writer Ales Rybak was born in 1934 in the village of Makavchitsky, Minsk Region. He is a graduate of the Byelorussian State University. His work first appeared in print in 1952. He is the author of collections of short stories and novels. Mr. Rybak now lives in Minsk. Diana Turner translated this story.

For readers who can't read...

Greek, Arabic, Chinese, Japanese, Dutch, Norwegian, Chukchi, Finnish, Hindi, Turkish, Urdu, Hebrew, Russian, Vietnamese, Portuguese, etc., etc.

Short Story International takes you to all points of the compass, to anywhere in the world. There are intriguing stories waiting for you in future issues of SSI—stories that will involve you in corners of this world you've never seen . . . and in worlds outside this one . . . with glimpses into the future as well as the past, revealing fascinating, universal truths that bypass differences in language and point up similarities in people.

Send in the coupon below and every other month SSI will take you on a world cruise via the best short stories being published throughout the world today—the best entertainment gleaned from the work of the great creative writers who are enhancing the oldest expression of the entertainment arts—the short story.

For the young people in your life. . .

The world of the short story for young people is inviting, exciting, rich in culture and tradition of near and far corners of the earth. *You* hold the key to this world. . .a world you can unlock for the young in your life. . .and inspire in them a genuine love for reading. We can think of few things which will give them as much lifelong pleasure as the habit of reading.

Seedling Series is directed to elementary readers (grades 4-7), and **Student Series** is geared to junior and senior high school readers.

Our stories from all lands are carefully selected to promote and strengthen the reading habit.

Give a Harvest of the World's Best Short Stories
Published Four Times a Year for Growing Minds.

Please enter subscription(s) to:

____ **Seedling Series: Short Story International**
$14. U.S. & U.S. Possessions
Canada $17 (U.S.) All Other Countries $19 (U.S.)

____ **Student Series: Short Story International**
$16. U.S. & U.S. Possessions
Canada $19 (U.S.) All Other Countries $21 (U.S.)

Mail with check to:
Short Story International
P.O. Box 405, Great Neck, N.Y. 11022

Donor: Name _____
Address _____
City _____State_____Zip_____
Country _____

Send to: Name _____
Address _____
City _____State_____Zip_____
Country _____
Please check ☐ New Subscription   ☐ Renewal

Send to: Name _____
Address _____
City _____State_____Zip_____
Country _____
Please check ☐ New Subscription   ☐ Renewal